# 1001
# CRANES

ALSO BY NAOMI HIRAHARA

ADULT FICTION

*Summer of the Big Bachi*
*Gasa-Gasa Girl*
*Snakeskin Shamisen*

# 1001 CRANES

## NAOMI HIRAHARA

DELACORTE PRESS

Published by Delacorte Press
an imprint of Random House Children's Books
a division of Random House, Inc.
New York

Delacorte Press and colophon are registered trademarks of Random House, Inc.

Visit us on the Web! www.randomhouse.com/kids
Educators and librarians, for a variety of teaching tools, visit us at
www.randomhouse.com/teachers

*Library of Congress Cataloging-in-Publication Data*
Hirahara, Naomi.
    1001 cranes / Naomi Hirahara.—1st ed.    p. cm.
    Summary: With her parents on the verge of separating, a devastated twelve-year-
old Japanese American girl spends the summer in Los Angeles with her
grandparents, where she folds paper cranes into wedding displays, becomes involved
with a young skateboarder, and learns how complicated relationships can be.
    ISBN 978-0-385-73556-8 (hardcover)—ISBN 978-0-385-90541-1 (lib. bdg.)
    1. Japanese Americans—Juvenile fiction. [1. Japanese Americans—Fiction.
2. Interpersonal relations—Fiction.   3. Marriage—Fiction.
4. Grandparents—Fiction.]   I. Title.   II. Title: One thousand and one cranes.
    PZ7.H59773Aam 2008    [Fic]—dc22    2007027655

The text of this book is set in 13-point Adobe Caslon.
Printed in the United States of America
10 9 8 7 6 5 4 3 2 1
First Edition

*To Martie, Sindy, and Coleen*

## ACKNOWLEDGMENTS

Special thanks to Sonia Pabley, Claudia Gabel, Random House and Delacorte Press, Bill and JoAnne Saito, Seinan Judo Dojo, Robert Kawahara, Lewis Kawahara and Akiko Takeshita, and Wes and Iesu, always Wes and Iesu.

### MICHI'S 1001-CRANES FOLDING TIP NO. 1:

Before you start, make sure your hands are clean.

# Monku with a Side of Smog

No *monku,* my dad tells me before my mother and I leave, but I think that it's easy for him to say. He's not the one going away.

"*Monku,*" which means "complaining" or "complain," is about the only Japanese word I know. And it may be the only Japanese word my parents know. But they make up for not knowing much Japanese by using "*monku*" all the time. Like when they told me that I couldn't go to a midnight concert with my friends: no *monku.* And when they told me that I couldn't quit piano lessons: no *monku.* And now about my going away for the summer: no *monku,* again.

My dad claims that we Katos don't *monku.* The rule doesn't apply to my mom. She's kept her maiden name; she'll forever be an Inui.

My first name is Angela, and I know that's no big deal, but if you consider who I'm named after, it might be. I got my name from an Angela who was on the FBI's Ten Most Wanted list back in the seventies. She's black and wore her Afro combed out like cotton candy. I know this only because I searched online for her one day. She's a radical, like my parents are, or maybe used to be. Now, don't get me wrong—my parents aren't hippies. They are too young to be real hippies; I guess they were involved in a second wave of hippiedom but aren't part of that world anymore. My dad, for example, is extra-neat, and my mom's always buying the latest deodorant to make sure her pits don't smell. They are both super-strict and limit the number of hours I can watch TV or surf the Internet. I don't even have a cell phone, even though my friends got theirs four years ago, when we were eight years old.

But in other ways, my parents are number-one rule breakers.

They met, in fact, at some kind of sit-in at Stanford, which pretty much means that they sat on the floor of the dean's office until they got their way, or at least thought they'd gotten their way. I think my dad was even arrested, though he won't admit it no matter how many times I ask. So it makes sense that Angela Davis was my parents' role model. Well, at least enough of one that they'd name their only kid after her.

My middle name is Michiko, after my maternal grandmother. My mother doesn't get along with her. My dad says it's because they're too much alike. I haven't made up my mind about Grandma Michi yet, because when I'm around her, she's always busy doing something else.

I've been to Grandma Michi and Gramps's house twelve times. I know this exact number because we go to Los Angeles once a year, during New Year's, which is important for Japanese people. My grandparents take us to the Buddhist temple near their house and we watch men use mallets to pound hot rice into this sticky goop they call *mochi*. Then the women, some of them wearing nets and caps over their hair, take the hot goop into the kitchen and spread it out on a floured wooden board. This next part is my favorite: we then tear the *mochi* with our fingers and make balls the size of eggs. The elderly ladies, including Grandma Michi, sit at a special table where they spoon red beans (actually, they are more brown) into the middle of the *mochi* and form the rice goop around them so the beans are a surprise in the middle. The red beans are called *an,* which sounds like when you open your mouth wide for the doctor. I think they taste better than chocolate. That's why Gramps calls me An-jay instead of Angie. I could eat *an* all day.

In five hours, we'll be seeing Gramps and Grandma Michi and it's not even close to New Year's. It's late June, summertime, when I'm supposed to be hanging out with my friends at home. Mill Valley, where we live, is just north of San Francisco, beyond the Golden Gate Bridge. Our house reminds me of a tree house, because it is surrounded by cedars, pines, and redwoods. My father teaches me the names of plants. He pulls the leaves off low branches and makes me smell and touch them. He says that even city girls need to know about green living things.

Now I close my eyes tight and picture the trees. When I open my eyes, I'm still in the backseat of our car; my mother is driving. It's just the two of us. My mother is pretty, I have to admit. A lot prettier than me. She doesn't quite look like those hula girls on the commercials for Hawaii vacations, but she comes close. Her nose goes up like an elf's, but her skin is smooth, without wrinkles and spots like other mothers have. While my hair is frizzy, like my dad's, her long hair falls straight, like a waterfall.

She doesn't care that she's up front by herself, because she gets to choose what CDs to play. She likes Sly and the Family Stone and all the Motown hits from the sixties and the seventies. "Real music," according to her. "Mom's Funk Junk Stuff," Dad used to call it. FJS, FJS. I can't remember the last time Dad teased Mom. I miss it.

"What do you think Daddy's doing now?" I ask Mom. It's Friday, and he usually doesn't work on Fridays.

Mom pushes out her lower jaw. "He's probably watching some replay of a game on TV."

I want to ask if he's at our house or his new apartment, but Mom may not even know about the apartment. I figured it out because the apartment manager called a couple of days ago and I answered the phone.

Even though I told the woman I'd give the message to my father, I didn't.

I first tried to write a note, but my fingers began to shake and I couldn't even hold on to a pen. Later the words got caught in my throat and never came out.

I don't know what this new apartment means. Dad has moved out before, but he's come back. For good, I thought until recently. I don't want to tell my mom about the phone call, because it might make everything worse. Maybe my dad's just thinking about it. I don't know.

I said nothing to my friends about my dad's possibly moving out again. Or about my parents' being in counseling together until my mother started going by herself. You see, there's another rule in our house: don't talk about bad things, especially in public. It's not a rule my parents have said out loud. But I know it in my heart.

I am so used to being quiet in groups that sometimes I forget how to talk in front of people I don't know well. This past school year, kids wrote things like "stay nice this summer" and "you're so nice" in my yearbook. Those words make me feel kind of strange, because I know I'm not that nice at all. It's just that they don't hear all the bad thoughts in my head.

I lean against my duffel bag, a giant formless stuffed animal, and stare out the window. There's nothing along the highway. Stretches of brown grass and dirt, like the underside of an old carpet that has been stripped from the floor. I can see rows of electrical transmission towers. Some look like metal outlines of cats on stilts or centipedes on their hind legs.

My mother drives slowly, so dusty cars pass us by, one by one. Some have only one person—the driver—but others are filled with families, bare feet, and mussed-up hair. Sleeping bags and bicycles are tied to the tops or the sides of vans. I wonder what it would be like in a car full of human noise. To feel the hot and stinky breath of the person next to you, to feel bare knees knocking against yours, elbows poking into your side, stickiness from either sweat or spilled soft drinks on the backs of your thighs. I doze off to Sly Stone's screaming, and then wake up to the worst smell filling my nostrils. We speed by a sign: KETTLEMAN CITY.

The windows of the car are all dusty and smeared with the brown and green guts of flying insects. But I can still make out the acres of white-and-black-splattered cows tightly crowded in mud.

Fumes of crap begin to rise in the Toyota.

"Mom, the vent, the vent."

My mother lowers the stereo volume and flips the vents closed. "Poor cows," she mutters.

I pinch my nose and take short breaths through my mouth.

"These animals are tough, Angela," my mother says, turning a knob to squirt soapy water onto the dirty windshield. "They can stand in their own crap."

All I can think is that at least they aren't alone.

# 2

# Sick Sadako

You know that Los Angeles is within striking distance when you reach the Grapevine. I have no idea why they call it the Grapevine. There are no vines of grapes, just boulders and hills and a special turnoff for trucks that can't handle the steep slopes. But my mother and I are going down the Grapevine, not up, which means the car isn't going to shudder or tremble as it often does on extreme inclines. We don't have to worry about overheating; we just have to make sure that we stay clear of any jackknifing trucks in the neighboring lane.

We clear a hill and then I see a few skyscrapers poking their heads out of some brown soup. Not quite the Emerald City. More like the rust city.

"We're going in there. . . ."

"It's not that bad. There's smog in northern Cal, too. Haven't you noticed it around San Jose?" my mother says.

It's going to take more than that for me to be sold on smog.

"Listen, I lived in smog for eighteen years. It didn't hurt me." She goes on to talk about the regular smog alerts they had in Gardena. The school alarm would go off and no one was allowed to go outside for recess. Instead of dodgeball, they played seven up, in which they put their heads down and stuck up their thumbs. Each of seven secret chosen ones would touch the thumb of someone whose head was down, and the thumbs would then disappear into fists. Then they all lifted their heads, and those with thumbs down guessed who had touched them.

She is talking again about the seventies, when all the Japanese girls used tape to create double eyelids, and feathered back their hair to look like Farrah Fawcett of *Charlie's Angels.* I have a feeling that this Scotch tape eyelid technique worked on my mother but not on my aunt Janet.

"Dad says smog smells bad." I remember exactly how he described it: tinny, like car exhaust mixed with nail polish. "He says that it also feels heavy. Like a rock on top of your chest."

"Dad doesn't know what he's talking about. He's not from L.A." My mother's voice sounds hollow, like a thick ceramic plate spinning on a linoleum floor. You're afraid the fallen plate is going to break, but it stays whole and empty at the same time.

"I don't think it's a good idea for me to be away all

summer," I tell Mom. I'm worried about what will happen while I'm gone.

"What are you talking about? Grandma and Gramps are expecting you. Janet and Grandma need your help. And you said you would go."

But that was before Mom started going to the counseling sessions alone, before Dad rented some apartment. My leaving was supposed to get them back together.

"So what's the big deal about this one-thousand-and-one-cranes stuff, anyway?" I ask.

"You saw the displays last New Year's, didn't you?"

All I can remember are the fancy black frames. I didn't spend too much time looking inside them. I was too busy stuffing my face with *an*, I guess.

"Well, they've since turned that back storage room they have into a one-thousand-and-one-cranes workroom."

"That many people want those things? What are they for, anyway? Good luck or something?"

"You know that book we used to read together— *Sadako and the Thousand Paper Cranes*?"

"Yeah, what about it?" I remember the story of Sadako, a young girl who suffered from radiation sickness caused by the atomic bomb. She started folding cranes and pretty soon everyone was making cranes so that she'd get better. As these things go, she just got worse and eventually died.

"Well, the Japanese fold a thousand cranes for

people to get better from sickness. I guess here in the States, the extra one is for good luck for weddings and anniversaries."

"You mean they don't even do this stuff in Japan?"

Mom shakes her head. "Not for weddings. I think it actually started in Hawaii."

"You and Dad didn't have a display, did you?" I try to remember the old photographs of their hippie wedding.

Mom takes a deep breath and I see her narrow shoulders tighten. "You know we're not into all that kind of stuff."

I sink back into my duffel bag. So Mom and Dad don't even believe in the displays. But they are going to force me to make them to earn my keep this summer. As we wind down the Grapevine, I picture myself hunched over a table, my fingers bleeding from 1001 paper cuts.

# 3

# Closed-mouth *Kokeshi*

Even though I've been to visit Gramps and Grandma twelve times, I never really paid attention to the house they lived in. Before, our visits would last, at the longest, a weekend. But I'm going to be there the whole summer. By myself.

So as my mother turns onto their street and parks the car in front of the house, I take a long, deep look. The paint is faded yellow, like sunshine that has just about quit. The house has a square cement porch with stairs and a peeling white wooden lattice on one side. The lawn is not the kind that tickles and soothes bare feet. Instead, it reminds me of the plastic grass at the miniature golf course near my other grandparents' house. The long driveway is cracked, with bits of stray gravel here and there.

I can't believe that my mother lived in such an ugly place.

"Angela, c'mon. Bring your stuff in." Mom holds open the back door, and I get out, dragging the duffel bag with me. The air is surprisingly cool and I even smell a tinge of salt.

Mom leaps over the two front stairs and raps on the screen door. No one answers, and I feel my head start to ache. I don't want to be here. I want to be with my dad, sitting on our deck, the sun shining through the trees onto our backs.

"Hmmm, I told them we'd be here around three o'clock." Mom tries to look through the windows, but heavy ivory drapes hide all evidence of what is inside. Finally, we hear the lock unlatch, and the door opens. Aunt Janet. "Oh, hello." Janet is rounder than I remembered, and through her white T-shirt and peasant skirt I can see that her belly is squishy and soft.

"Where is everybody?" Mom never bothers to say "hi" or "goodbye" to Aunt Janet, I've noticed.

"At the shop. We have a wedding tonight. I just dropped off the crane display."

My mother glances down at her watch. "I've got to go to the bank before it closes. Angela, you stay with Aunt Janet."

"I'll go with you."

"No, you stay. It'll be better. You must be tired, anyway."

"I'm not that tired," I lie.

"No, Angela, you're staying here."

From the tone of her voice, I know that my mother is

going to do something she doesn't want me to see. Something I'm sure involves my dad.

"Maybe I'll go skateboarding." I know that idea isn't going to fly with Mom.

"You will not. You will stay inside the house with Aunt Janet." Mom presses her fingers into the flesh of my upper arm and it hurts. I drop my duffel bag. She then pushes me through the front door. I bump into Aunt Janet, who almost falls backward, causing her gold-rimmed granny glasses to lie lopsided on her face. "Janet will show you where you're staying, so you can settle in."

I feel the whole top half of my face grow hot. My nose becomes runny, as if I have just swallowed a big dollop of wasabi.

Mom goes back to the porch to retrieve my duffel bag and drops it just inside the door. "I'll be back," she says. "It'll only take an hour or so." She then looks at me as if to say "sorry," but I keep my head down.

I rub the spot where she grabbed me, my arm outstretched as if I've just given blood. I stay in that awkward position for a few minutes, until I hear the door of the car open and shut and the engine turn on. Meanwhile, Janet fixes her glasses so that they lie exactly perpendicular to her knot of a nose. She closes the door, bends down to pick up the duffel bag, and places the bag by the sofa.

I stare at two Japanese masks hanging beside the door. One, a hideous demon face with horns and a menacing grin, is made out of wood. The eyes are life-like; the mask's creator even carved out the dark of his pupils. Next to the demon is the white face of a woman, her skin the color of the ashy end of a cigarette. She smiles sweetly and her eyes slope down like two commas on their sides. I don't know which mask is spookier; even though the woman is smiling, she's probably not smiling on the inside.

"You must be thirsty. How about some Coke?" Aunt Janet gestures toward a television inside a fake-wood console in the living room. "You can watch TV. Or play solitaire on the computer."

I shake my head.

"You'll be in your mom's old room, but we haven't had time to clean it just yet. Tonight you and your mom will have to stay in the living room on the couch. I hope that's okay. It'll be like a slumber party."

Yeah, I think. The last person I want sleeping next to me is my mother.

"Sit down. Sit down, Angie. Please."

I stay by the door for a moment, just to spite her. But there is something about her lumpy figure that softens my hard edges.

I go into the living room and sit on the couch. The living room is the opposite of our tidy one up north. The Inui house isn't dirty, but overfilled, like a small man who has eaten too much. At any time, the room could belch or vomit its contents, like an active volcano.

Grandma Michi and Gramps don't like to think in

ones. They think instead in twos, fours, and sixes. There isn't only one rooster knickknack marking Gramps's birth in the year of the rooster, but four of them in different sizes and made of different materials, next to a black grizzly bear statue with a clock in its middle; six dancing Japanese dolls; and at least eight *kokeshi* dolls, the skinny wooden ones with no arms or legs. What freaks me out about those—as well as Hello Kitty—is that they have no mouths. They can't eat or smile or talk.

On each side of the fireplace are four built-in white brick cubbyholes stuffed with household items—plastic soda holders, wooden boards that were attached to bright pink fish cakes called *kamaboko,* toilet paper cardboard rolls. Why does Grandma Michi hold on to junk? It makes me feel anxious and sad at the same time.

"Coke?" Aunt Janet brings a glass of soda with ice cubes and places it on a crocheted coaster on the coffee table. The table is already stained with countless circles, so I don't know what good the coaster is.

I take a sip and feel the fizz go up my nose. I wish I could spend all afternoon inhaling, feeling bubbles and not much else. But carbonation doesn't work like that. It doesn't last forever.

On the wall across from the couch are about a dozen framed photographs of the family. The only black-and-white one is of Gramps and Grandma's wedding. Gramps was so handsome then, his jet-black hair oiled and combed back. The line of his nose reminds me of the marking of an extra-sharp pencil. He looked like he could have been a scientist. Grandma, on the other hand, had a bigger build than she does now; you can even see it through her white satin dress. She had broad shoulders, like a football player, as well as a broad face. She reminds me of a bear, not a scary grizzly or a soft stuffed teddy bear, but something in between. There was a deep wrinkle at the top of her nose, a secret zipper; if you tugged at it, ghouls and ghosts would tumble out, telling stories of what it was like to be held captive in Grandma Michi's head.

In the center of the wall is a family photo, a little crooked, taken at least twelve years later. Gramps and Grandma, looking a little worn around the edges—hair thinner and wrinkles by their eyes and mouths—with my mom and Aunt Janet. Even though Aunt Janet is only three years older than Mom, at eight years old she looked like she outweighed Mom by fifty pounds. I've always wanted a brother or a sister but I don't know what I would do if I had a mini Mom. Aunt Janet does not seem to mind. She is oblivious that Mom is ten times smarter and more beautiful.

I can't make out a small photo in the corner, and I rise to get a closer look. It's Aunt Janet in a red cowboy hat, with Gramps, in dark glasses, kneeling beside her. They must have been at a petting zoo, because a goat was nibbling off the brim of Janet's cowboy hat. Aunt

Janet was daddy's little girl and so am I. That is one of the few things we have in common.

"Cute," I say. "You looked real cute back then." My cheeks flush as I realize how mean that sounds, but Janet doesn't seem to mind.

"TV?"

I shake my head.

"Do you want to see our new one-thousand-and-one-cranes room?" For a split second, it looks as if Aunt Janet's eyes become darker and more expansive. She's excited, more excited than I've ever seen her.

"All right," I say, placing the soda glass on the coaster.

I follow Aunt Janet through a narrow hallway to a rectangular room that used to be their storage room. It is just as cluttered as the rest of the house and almost cavelike. Then I see them along the wall: the 1001-cranes displays. Hundreds of gold and silver folded cranes shine against black backgrounds like minerals in a dark, deep mine. And when I get closer, I can see the individual cranes, flat against each other like scales of a golden fish.

"There's a saying: 'If one crane has a hundred years of life, a thousand cranes will have a million years of life.' So maybe all these marriages will last a million years."

I look back at Aunt Janet and she has a goofy grin on her face. Even though she's old, she has no clue about the real world.

The cranes are arranged in all sorts of designs. Japanese writing. A butterfly beginning to bat its wings. A snowcapped mountain. Flowers and leaves open to the sky. The cranes are all metallic, except for a red one glued to the bottom of each display.

There's a pile of loose origami cranes gleaming like gold coins in a pirate's stash on top of two folding tables next to a row of glue containers.

"Careful," Aunt Janet says as I pick up one of the cranes. "Are your hands clean?"

I drop it back into its pile and Aunt Janet lets out a noise that is something between a laugh and a relieved sigh. "Oh, that's a B crane. Never mind."

"Huh?"

"We grade them—A, B, and C. The Bs and Cs go on the bottom, where you can't see them as much."

Aunt Janet then points to a row of black-framed images against the other side of the wall. The poor Cs are the cranes that are mostly covered with layers of the As and the Bs. If I was graded, I would be labeled a C—something that goes in the background.

I'm amazed that my aunt Janet and Grandma Michi take so much time to glue all these origami birds together.

"I don't get it," I say. "Why don't you open the birds up?"

The best thing about making an origami crane is pulling at its wings and puffing up its middle. In one stroke, you give life to a bird. It changes from two-dimensional to three-dimensional. Why would they want to keep the cranes flat?

"Silly," Aunt Janet says. "How can you frame it? Lasts longer this way."

I'm getting the idea that I've entered a different world. I can hold on to my Mill Valley world or I can let go to fully enter this new one.

"That one says *'kotobuki,'* or 'longevity,' " Janet says, referring to cranes assembled in the shape of some Japanese writing, strokes bringing to mind a man pulling his left leg in after kicking.

"Longevity," I repeat. "It looks Chinese, like those things they have on the wall of a Chinese restaurant."

"Same characters," Janet explains. "The Japanese call their writing *kanji.* Those others are of *mon,* family crests."

"Neat," I say. "What's our crest?"

"Well, you get it from your mother's side, so we're not quite sure. Mom's family doesn't have good records like Dad's."

I study the images for a while.

"You've done origami before?" Aunt Janet asks.

"In elementary school." I did a few origami cranes back then, but I never really got the hang of it. I've also done my share of paper airplanes since then with my dad, but I don't think that counts.

"Oh yeah, and fortune-tellers," I say, remembering.

My friends in Mill Valley love origami, and in grade school we all made fortune-tellers out of blue-lined paper. You'd put your fingers in the slots, say a quick incantation, and then have another girl make her selection. Underneath the folded triangle would be her fortune. The good girls would write *You're going to marry a really cute guy,* or *You're super-nice.* But my friends and I created fortunes that read *You're going to marry a geek,* and *You're going to fall into a hole and die.*

"You'll learn soon enough. Mom will teach you."

I would prefer for Aunt Janet to teach me instead, but I don't say anything. Aunt Janet holds out a booklet to me. I notice for the first time that her fingers are strangely shaped, splayed out, with large flat nails shaped like mini clamshells. "Here, you might want to take a look at this."

MICHI'S 1001-CRANES FOLDING TIPS, the cover reads. The simple black-and-white booklet is photocopied and stapled. It is typewritten, with a few hand-drawn diagrams of how best to fold an origami crane.

I read the first tip: *Before you start, make sure your hands are clean.*

I start to feel scared. Grandma Michi and Aunt Janet take this all very seriously. What will happen if I mess up?

I return the booklet to the table and walk away, dragging my finger along the plastic sleeves and the covers of photo albums stacked there. In the corner, like a brilliant exotic flower from Hawaii or a gigantic flame, are strings of multicolored cranes, all open and in flight.

"Ooooh, I like this one," I say, turning back to Aunt Janet. "All the colors. The cranes aren't so smashed up like those in the frames. And the wings are open."

"I made that for your parents. When they got married."

"Mom said that she wasn't into origami cranes."

"She probably forgot. I mean, it was such a long time ago. I don't think Japanese Americans were really even doing them much for weddings back then. Well, maybe in Hawaii."

"It's not even dusty."

"I clean it every week. With a feather duster."

Somehow, hearing that makes me both happy and sad. Happy that someone cares about my mom and dad's being together. And sad because it seems like we are actually falling apart in three separate pieces.

"They're pretty, but you can't really see the cranes too well. It's like they disappear with all the other ones," she says, adjusting her glasses. "But this has a thousand and one cranes—exactly. Some people cheat, you know. They use fewer than a thousand and one. But I keep an exact count."

"So what would happen if it wasn't exact?"

Aunt Janet hesitates, and her lips part for a moment, so I know she is irritated. "Well, it wouldn't be right," she says.

The back door of the 1001-cranes room opens, and

there is Grandma, her hands full of paper bags and boxes. Aunt Janet rushes over to help her while I stay behind with the multicolored crane display.

Grandma looks the same as when I saw her at New Year's. Only now her hair is a uniform chestnut brown. In December, she had patches of gray, like a worn clapboard whose paint was peeling. The entire barn has now been repainted, yet it looks a bit odd, fake. I almost prefer the worn clapboard.

Her mouth seems different, too. Grandma has heavy lines that extend below the two ends of her disappearing lips, making the bottom of her face look a little like a marionette's. But today she has drawn fat lips onto her flat mouth, a crimson butterfly.

"You're here," she says. "Hungry?"

# 4

# Bedtime for An-jay

I am taking a bite of my chicken teriyaki when I hear Grandma whispering to Aunt Janet in the corner of the kitchen. "Where did she go?"

"Something about the bank."

"Good, good."

Grandma's voice is strange, like she's an FBI agent.

I hear the front door open and shut and expect to feel the frenetic birdlike energy of my mother. Instead, it is the graceful movement of Gramps. He comes from behind and squeezes my shoulders. "An-jay, you're still skin and bones."

I laugh when I hear Gramps's voice. I'm actually not that skinny compared to the stick girls at school, but I don't correct him.

"You smell like flowers," I say. I swish some chicken in the sauce at the bottom of the Styrofoam container.

"So what's going on? Your mom causing havoc as

usual?" Gramps has permanent lines on his forehead, only made deeper when he smiles.

"She's not here."

"She's not?"

Gramps then disappears through the swinging doors of the kitchen. Those doors remind me of an old-time Western saloon in the cowboy movies Gramps likes to watch.

Mom reappears about thirty minutes later. After hugging Gramps, she sits with Grandma at the dining room table, papers in hand. It's odd for them to get along so well, and I'm suspicious.

Aunt Janet escapes to the 1001-cranes room while Gramps and I sit in the overstuffed living room, watching a rerun of a TV crime show and sucking on Funyuns, fake onion rings from a bag. Before the cops arrive on the scene, Gramps is fast asleep.

During the quiet parts of the show, I hear Grandma talking to Mom. "Get a lawyer," she says.

"I am a lawyer."

"You know what I'm saying. Get one who specializes."

A commercial comes on and I can't hear Mom's response.

They start talking about numbers, bank accounts, and withdrawals. I think I hear Mom cursing Dad a few times. Later on, they begin talking about me.

"She's still doing well in English—I mean, she's always doing well in English. But she almost failed math.

She used to be good in math. And social studies, too. I'm thinking that it might be her friends."

"Don't worry," Grandma says. "We'll straighten her out."

I don't like the words or the tone of their voices. Grandma is talking about me as if I am a crooked hanger or a crumpled-up piece of paper. And what is Mom saying?

She's the one, after all, who thinks that everything about my grandparents and Aunt Janet is old and stale. Janet is still best friends with her best friends from high school, Mom says, laughing. It's only a matter of time before grocery stores and big warehouse stores kill my Gramps's flower business. Dead-end business, my mother says. Dead-end lives.

But in spite of what she says and thinks, she is still going to leave me here with Aunt Janet, Grandma, and Gramps. And the 1001 cranes, for better or worse.

When the TV episode ends and the news comes on, Gramps shifts in his easy chair and finally stands up.

"Bedtime for An-jay," he declares, and then retrieves a couple of pillows from the linen closet.

We open up a sleeping bag, musty and fishy-smelling from a camping trip that was decades ago, but somehow that smell comforts me. The inside lining has rows of elk and rabbits grazing in a forest by a lake. I imagine that the scene is somewhere in northern California, and try to tell myself that Dad has changed his mind and decided not to move out after all. After I tuck myself into the sleeping bag on the floor, Gramps puts up his hand—it's not even a wave, really—and disappears into the hallway to his bedroom.

It is almost an hour later when I hear Mom saying good night to Grandma. Mom snaps off the light and then stumbles over to the couch. I stir so that she'll know I am still awake.

"Can't sleep?" she asks.

"Feels strange in here."

She struggles with the zipper of her sleeping bag, which Gramps and I laid out on the couch, and finally gets in, not even bothering to take off her jeans.

"It won't be so bad," she finally says. "I'll come down as much as I can."

"How about Dad?"

"Angie, please, not that again."

"You mean, I won't get to see him the whole summer?"

"He'll call you. Probably every day, even."

"He didn't call today."

"Well, today doesn't count, because you saw him this morning."

He was in his favorite pair of torn Stanford sweatpants, which he wears to bed every night. He hugged me hard and tousled my hair. His unshaved face felt like sandpaper against my cheek. He's not like those Asian men with thin rattail mustaches; he can grow a full beard in a matter of days. "Don't cause any trouble down there in L.A. And remember: no *monku*."

He said the stuff about *monku* as our special code, I realize deep down inside. No matter how surrounded I would be by Inuis, I was still a Kato, he was reminding me.

"It's going to go by so quickly, Angie. The summer's going to be over before you know it," Mom says. Then she turns onto her side, her back toward me. The streetlight outside bleeds a thin line of silver onto the wall above the drapes, and I see the outline of Mom's narrow shoulders, first tight and still, and then rising and falling, ever so slightly, matching the beat of her breath.

# 5

# Poisoned Phone

She's ready to go when I wake up the next morning. Seeing her freshly washed hair and her car keys in her hand makes me feel desperately lonely.

"It's just for the summer," she reminds me again. "It'll be best. For everyone. Really."

I now feel like kicking and screaming and telling my mom not to leave me here. But instead I nod as Gramps, Grandma, and Aunt Janet stand by the door.

I have been taught well. No *monku*. I stand in front of my mother and let her briefly embrace me, her chin cutting into the soft fold of my neck.

"I have something for you," she then says, revealing a red cell phone in her hand. "An early birthday present." It's as shiny as a fresh candy apple. I don't like red. My mother knows that. She must have bought the phone in a hurry. Or else she wasn't thinking.

"I've already programmed my cell phone number.

And your father's." Two different numbers, two separate lives.

I wave good-bye from the sidewalk. After the car turns the corner, I take a big breath through my nose. And then another and another. But no matter how hard I try, I cannot smell the smog.

MICHI'S 1001-CRANES FOLDING TIP NO. 2:
Select an origami paper with a color that is
vibrant, bright, and hard to miss. Gold and
silver are the best.

# 6

# Three Kinds of *Kami*

I know that there's not just one kind of grandma. I know this because I met Nana, the grandmother of my best friend, Emilie, when she was visiting from New York City. Nana's hair was short—real short, like a businessman's—and as white as a polar bear's coat. She wore huge round earrings from Africa and brightly colored clothes that had no zippers or buttons. When she spoke to us, she got right in our faces; the rims of her red-framed glasses almost hit our cheeks. She wanted to know everything about us—whether we'd had boyfriends (Emilie, yes, for two weeks; and me, no, never), whether our school taught sex education, and whether we regularly read (Emilie, no, except for celebrity magazines; and me, yes, especially manga). She kept telling us that girls needed to learn skills and make money; they couldn't depend on men, and besides, women outlived men. Emilie was totally embarrassed, but I thought Nana was funny. After that first interrogation, Emilie made sure her nana never ever met her friends again.

I've also had firsthand experience with my grandma on the Kato side, my dad's mom. My cousins and I call her Baa-chan—yeah, like a sheep crying out to another sheep. My grandpa on that side is called Jii-chan. Jii-chan and Baa-chan live in the East Bay near Berkeley. Baa-chan's fingers are kind of bent, but she doesn't let that stop her from pinching my arms and cheeks. She buys me stuff all the time, but she keeps the price tags on everything, because she knows that her taste isn't the same as mine.

Even though we call her Baa-chan, Dad's mom knows nothing about Japan. Nothing. She and Jii-chan, have a Japanese scroll in their living room and sometimes she wears clothing made of kimono material, but she always tells us, "I'm pure USA, born and bred. Hundred percent American."

If you're 100 percent, I think, why are we calling you Baa-chan? And why did you beat all that *monku* stuff into Dad's head?

Grandma Michi is really different from Baa-chan. She never touches me unless it's to push me along so I'll walk faster. She doesn't tell us stories about living on a farm and catching rabbits in the summertime. I don't really know anything about Grandma Michi.

But Grandma Michi does know a lot about Japan. I asked her once if she had ever lived there, and she gave me a long, cold look, as if I had accused her of being a Nazi. "No, never," she said, barely looking at me.

*Then how come you know so much?* I wanted to ask her. That's how it is with Grandma Michi. It's like you're walking in a minefield and you don't know when the bombs might go off right underneath you. That's why I've learned to keep quiet and watch.

Right now Grandma Michi has me sitting at the counter at Gramps's flower shop. She has spent the past hour talking all about 1001 cranes. Some of it is actually interesting.

She explains to me that the tradition of a thousand cranes goes back to a long time ago, when Japanese people walked around with samurai swords.

"Origami" is the combination of two words: *"ori,"* meaning "to fold," and *"gami,"* "paper." "But *'gami'* is really *'kami,'*" she explains. "When the Japanese say 'paper,' they say *'kami,'* not *'gami.'*"

"Well, why don't they just say 'orikami'?" I ask.

"Sometimes when they combine, they change the sounds a little so it's easier to say the word. But *'kami'* can also mean 'hair' or it can mean 'god.' So you have to be careful."

Careful of what? I wonder. It isn't like I'm going to be walking around saying "I want a piece of *kami* to write on. I need to brush my *kami*. *Kami* bless you." I don't dare verbalize my thoughs, because Grandma isn't the type to take kindly to jokes. And she is in an especially bad mood right now.

I am having my first crane-folding lesson in the flower shop, the 1001 cranes' "first base of business," Grandma tells me. This is where we snag most of our new customers. If they need flowers for their wedding or anniversary, they often need a 1001-cranes display. Back at the house is where we make the displays.

My lesson with Grandma is not going well. She has created a D pile and even an F pile for the ones that don't make her cut.

"Always match the edges. You can't go wrong if you go from there," Grandma Michi says, peering over my elbow. "And no white should show," she repeats for the tenth time, as if revealing white is as bad as letting someone see your underwear.

Why don't they just make origami paper that is colored on both sides, instead of leaving one side white? That would get rid of the "white" problem for sure.

The most boring part of origami is making folds and then unfolding them. "Now you have guiding lines," Grandma says. From these lines you can flip the paper and make more complicated folds. So it begins: fold the square piece of paper in half, like a sandwich, and then open. Fold it in half in the other direction and then open. Then it starts to get a little trickier: fold two diagonal corners together to form a triangle, open, and do the same with the other corners. All the while, watch those edges and make sure the white doesn't show. Grandma is fanatical about the folded corners. They have to be as sharp as the point of a knife. If they aren't, the cranes are thrown into the D pile or the F pile to go straight to crane hell.

Once the guiding lines are created, the hard part comes. You have to fold all the insides into each other to create a smaller square that opens up like a flower. As I flip the paper and make all the folds and corners, I feel as though my belly is going through the same strange movements.

I am attempting my eleventh bird—an F—when the bell attached to the top of the door rings. A customer has come to pick up arrangements for a fund-raiser. "I'll need to help him load up his van," Grandma Michi says to me, wiping her hands on her apron. "Watch the shop for me, all right?"

Before I can *monku*, Grandma disappears into the back room and goes out the back door. I sigh and study the dreary storefront. Linoleum squares, in a pattern of swirled tan and white like cold coffee with curdled cream, line the floor. The shop is really clean—Grandma makes sure of that—but still it seems crowded.

One metal stand holds greeting cards: "Happy Anniversary," "Happy Birthday," "Get Well," and, of course, "In Sympathy." Gramps's customers must be into sickness and death, because there are more of those cards than anything else. They are all depressing, no cartoon characters or bright colors. Instead, they feature stiff irises or ugly lilies that look fake and especially out of place in a flower shop.

On the opposite side of the store, next to the counter,

is a long freezer with a sliding glass door. Inside are Grandpa's masterpieces; I understand why people travel far for his arrangements. A dozen perfect roses in a glass vase. The long stems, smooth and thornless, are straight as needles and positioned as carefully as fake-pearl pins in a bride's fancy hairdo. Each bud is partly open, a beautiful woman's red lips. Another arrangement is more fun: blue flowers, with edges like baby bonnets, placed underneath a spray of white-shaped bells and dazzled with daisies, each petal outstretched as if happy to be alive—at least for now. In the corner is a Hawaiian number, tropicals that look like an exotic display of animals: bright orange beaks, the furry nose of a woolly mammoth, and red feathery crowns.

The wooden counter I sit at is worn and smooth, probably from all the times my grandparents have slid floral arrangements across it to their customers. Gramps keeps his tools neatly to one side, in a shoe box. A funny circular metal tool that wraps around stems of roses to dethorn them. Green floral tape. Pruning shears. Stacked beside the box are two photo albums— one of flower arrangements, and the other of 1001-cranes displays.

To keep my folded cranes clean, Grandma makes me use a large cutting board that looks like it has been pulled from the counter in someone's kitchen. I'm not quite sure if my efforts are just practice or will be used in someone's 1001-cranes display. With the edge of my fingernail, I crease the folded square and then fold the sides to meet a line in the middle. The resulting shape resembles a gold kite waiting to be released in the wind.

The bell rings again, and I expect to see Grandma. Instead, it's a black girl a little younger than me. She's swimming in a white martial arts outfit that looks like a canvas robe and pants. There's an orange belt around her middle. Her hair is puffy yet neat—like two loaves of french bread braided together.

"You're Auntie Michi's granddaughter," she says.

Auntie Michi? I can't imagine Grandma Michi ever being an "auntie." First of all, she doesn't have any sisters or brothers that I know of. And second of all, I picture aunties as being soft and gentle, smelling of perfume. Definitely not Grandma Michi.

I wait to see if the girl is going to buy something, but from the way she walks around, I know that she's just here to waste time. I ignore her and concentrate on my latest crane. I take the kite shape and bend the top of it down. A couple of swift swipes of the fingernail to ensure a sharp line, and then open it all up again to the folded square. Now is the toughest challenge, tougher than anything that has come before: lift the bottom corner to form the shape of a baby bird's open mouth, and finally, close to a diamond shape. Half of the diamond is slit in half, and I know that the slit needs to face the bottom. Fold the sides to the middle again. These folds are not guiding lines but one step from the finale. I have the head and the tail now; I just need to fold up and then in. With my last two cranes, I was bogged down by an F-rated lumpy head or crooked tail, but this one is different. The neck of the crane remains elegant and straight, its folded head demurely lowered. Where is Grandma? I have just folded a perfect crane, worthy of the A pile. I lay it delicately on its side on the wooden cutting board.

"Not bad," the girl says, and takes one of my origami papers. Her slender fingers then move back and forth quickly, as if she's knitting the paper with her bare hands. And then, voilà—a perfectly formed grade-A crane.

I sit here, stunned. This pint-sized karate kid knows her origami.

"I was going to help Michi with the one-thousand-and-one-cranes displays. But that was before you came along."

I narrow my eyes. I can't say that I'm a big fan of Grandma Michi, but she still is *my* grandmother, not this girl's.

"Why are you dressed in a karate outfit?" I finally ask. It's not like me to speak to strangers like that, but I feel she is challenging me.

"It's not karate; it's judo. And it's called a *gi*." She sticks out her front teeth (she has a slight overbite anyway) and spits out the last word. "My dad works at the dojo around the corner sometimes."

I look at her blankly and she sighs. "Do-jo. It's a place where we learn judo."

I know what she's getting at: I'm the Japanese person, so I should know all this stuff. But I don't, and I'm kind of proud that I don't. Like I'm a little bit like Baa-chan right now, with her American flag pin that she sometimes wears.

The bell rings, and Grandma steps in, sweat running down the sides of her face like clear liquid sideburns. She looks dazed for a moment, as if she has been exposed to the sun too quickly.

She then takes note of the white-uniformed girl in the store and smiles. "Oh, so you've met my favorite little helper, I see," she says.

# 7

# Eggs, Ketchup, and Shoyu

Grandma Michi's little helper has a name. It's Rachel Joseph. I've made up my mind that I don't like Rachel Joseph. I don't care that Grandma Michi calls the girl her favorite, but it's obvious that Rachel Joseph does. I can tell by how she smiles, her upper teeth all jammed in her small jaw. She likes to be called Grandma Michi's favorite. That's fine, I think. You can wear that crown.

"I'd like you to be nice to Rachel," Grandma Michi says as we are driving home.

I'm surprised that my grandmother is still thinking about that little judo girl.

"I'm nice," I say, knowing that it really isn't true. But how did Grandma Michi figure that out so quickly?

"Sometimes she likes to sit in the shed in back of the shop, next to the Dumpster. It's a playhouse for her. She knows the combination to the lock."

Whatever, I think. If she wants to hang out in a probably rat-infested shack, it's her business.

When I get back to the house with Grandma Michi, I check to see if Dad has called. But he hasn't.

"Are you sure the answering machine is working? Looks pretty old." Their message machine has two minicassettes—one for outgoing messages, the other for incoming—and I flip up the lid to make sure the tape for incoming is still intact.

"No messages for you, Angela," Janet repeats. "I checked, two times." She flutters her single eyelids, her straight lashes pointed downward like the brushes of a vacuum cleaner. "What about your cell phone?"

I haven't touched my phone since Mom gave it to me this morning. If it was any other time, I would be checking out all the features and text-messaging my friends in Mill Valley. But somehow, the cell phone makes me mad. Like it's a bribe for me to behave myself. I do want to hear from Dad, so I finally open it up and check for messages. Nothing. Maybe Dad doesn't even have my number. I wait for a little while and call his cell. The voice mail picks up. My heart first jumps at the sound of his voice and then feels heavy. I think about leaving a message but hang up before the recording gets to the beep.

Before I go to bed tonight, I walk over to the two masks beside the door. I focus on the face of the smiling woman. *What are you so happy about?* I ask her silently.

And why is your face so pale? I'll never understand why being the color of plaster is considered beautiful in Japan.

The more I stare at the mask, the more confused I become about her expression. Is she really laughing? Or maybe crying? Or both.

I sleep in the sleeping bag again, this time on the couch, where my mother slept the night before. When Gramps wakes me up to eat on Sunday, it is nine o'clock. Grandma and Aunt Janet have already left to deliver a 1001-cranes display to a wedding.

"I can do breakfast real good. In camp I worked in the mess hall," Gramps says. The camp he's talking about is not summer camp, but a camp in the swampland in Arkansas where he and his family were locked up during World War II for being Japanese. I don't know why anyone would have mistaken Gramps for being real Japanese— that is, born in Japan. He speaks hardly any Japanese, and his favorite television shows are all-American westerns, although a lot of times he has seemed to root for the Indians more than the cowboys.

He breaks four eggs, two in each hand, against the edge of the skillet, lines of egg whites dripping onto the stove top. He is all thumbs, but I can't blame him for trying to cheer me up.

"Set the table, will you, An-jay? And don't forget the ketchup. And the shoyu."

I'm not quite sure what Gramps is preparing for breakfast, but I am too tired to ask. In Mill Valley, we usually eat fresh raspberries and blueberries over granola with soy milk. What appear here are two runny sunny-side up eggs over fried bologna and a side of rice.

"You eat rice for breakfast?"

"Doesn't everyone?" Gramps says, squirting ketchup on his eggs and then dousing them with soy sauce. "In fact, I betcha most of the world eats this stuff."

My stomach starts to turn and I take a sip of orange juice.

Gramps notices that I'm not eating. "You've been living up in that *hakujin* town too long."

Whenever I'm with Gramps, he inevitably starts his *hakujin* talk. His universe is clearly defined for him: the Japanese world and the *hakujin*, white, world.

"I have a black friend at school," I say.

"But I bet she's *hakujin* inside."

I roll my eyes. When Gramps gets into this mode, there's no talking to him.

"So what are you going to do today? I was thinking of fixing Janet's old bike for you."

"I brought my skateboard."

"Skateboard? Isn't that what those crazy *hakujin* boys do?"

My skateboard, an old concave wooden deck with four tan polyurethane wheels, is nothing special. But it's my main source of independent transportation and I am planning to go as far as it will take me.

"Well, don't go too far," Gramps says. "Gardena isn't what it used to be." In spite of his reservations, he takes an old shoelace threaded through a key and places it around my neck. "Put that underneath your shirt, so no one can see," he says.

I do as I am told, feeling the coldness of the key against my breastbone above my bra. It is one of those bras with molded cups, 34A. In the crisscross intersection is a tiny embroidered pink flower sitting in the middle of a green fabric leaf.

I don't make it past the lawn before I hear someone calling to me from the driveway next door. It is a Japanese woman about my grandmother's age. "Hello there. Hello. You must be Michi and Nick's granddaughter. I'm Ruth Oyama and this is my husband, Jack."

Mr. Oyama holds a black Bible; Mrs. Oyama's Bible is in a quilted book cover with handles. My family isn't religious, so I always am both curious about and repelled by people who go to church. Certain Christian people's faces seem especially bright, like they are shining a light into the dark corners of my mind. The lady, Mrs. O, has a piercing gaze, and I feel that she can see right through me.

"Oh," I finally say, realizing that they are waiting for me to introduce myself. I drop my skateboard onto the driveway. "I'm Angela. Angela Kato."

"Kato . . . Your dad related to the Katos in San Gabriel?" Mr. Oyama asks.

I crinkle my nose and nudge my skateboard with the toe of my sneaker. "I don't know. My dad's from northern California," I say.

"We're going to be late, Jack. It was so nice to meet you, Angela. I'm sure we'll be seeing you again."

I wait until they pull their Honda out of the driveway and into the street. Mrs. O turns and waves to me. I look down, hoping that I have dodged the light.

As soon as they leave, I race down the street on my skateboard.

For the first time in several days, I feel totally free.

# 8

# Mixed-up Mon

Gardena is flat and unadorned; nothing looks organic or particularly wild. The buildings and the three-bedroom ranch homes seem snapped into place like pieces of Lego.

I stand on my skateboard, and with some quick thrusts of my right foot, I am rolling down the concrete road. The pavement is rough, full of cracks and holes, and the ride is jerky, as well. I turn a couple of corners, move over to the sidewalk, and then approach a business district. There is a series of small storefronts squished together like friends conspiring to keep secrets. Only the Mexican pastry shop seems interesting, and as I roll past, I almost bump into a middle-aged woman doing her weekend shopping.

I have about a dollar in my pocket, so I go to a corner liquor store and buy some sour gummy worms. Bright blue, orange, red, and yellow, they are tart enough to make me cringe.

I go down more streets; I don't recognize the trees growing beside the sidewalks, and their unfamiliarity upsets me. Instead of being heavy and full, they look a bit stunted, controlled. Smog trees, I call them, and begin to feel better. The smog trees, deformed like something inside me, could be my friends.

I'm looking at some of them when I arrive at a neat black wrought iron fence that comes up to my chin. Behind it are two giant cement Japanese lanterns and a huge structure with a sloped roof. The Buddhist church. Although I've been here twelve times before, the white building seems kind of new to me. I notice a pretty crest—called a *mon*, I remember—right below where the two sides of the roof meet. *Mon* seem always to be inside of circles. This *mon* looks like two flattened furry fern leaves tied together.

I skateboard down a large boulevard and then can see a big overpass and a school. The school, a wallflower attempting to blend in and be unnoticed, is a nondescript tan. Beyond the main building is an open yard with outdoor basketball, handball, and tetherball courts and picnic tables. And a dozen skateboarders.

Some merely circle the tetherball courts. The more adventurous ones sail down the stairs or grind their wooden decks down metal railings.

I'm watching them from the other side of a chain-link fence when one of the skateboarders finally rolls toward me. A guy, kind of cute, maybe thirteen. He wears a white T-shirt and an open yellow plaid shirt. He has long dark-brown hair that curls up a little. As he gets closer, I notice that he has sideburns and a light mustache.

"Hey," he says. He kicks up his skateboard and I see the huge skull image on its deck.

I look down and tighten my grip on my skateboard. My fingers are still sticky from the gummy worms. "Hello."

"Are those OJs?"

"Huh?"

"Your wheels. They look like Santa Cruz OJs. They're classic. From the eighties."

"No," I say, "they're just regular ones. Your skateboard's nice." I blush at how stupid that sounds.

"You go to this school?"

I shake my head. "I'm from Mill Valley."

The skateboarder frowns.

"It's near San Francisco."

"You're pretty far from San Francisco."

"I'm staying with my grandparents. Not far from here."

"Cool. Come out with us." He grasps the chain-link fence and I notice that his knuckles look knotty and his fingernails have fine white lines on them.

I'm not wearing a watch, but I know that it's late. I shake my head. "I have to get going."

"Well, next week, then. We're here every Sunday afternoon." He backs up and begins walking toward his friends. I reposition my head so that I can place the boy in one of the diamonds in the fence.

"Hey," he says, turning back. "What's your name?"

"Angie," I say, and he turns his side to me, signaling that he has not heard me, his hand cupping his ear.

"Angie," I yell in a strange voice that doesn't sound like mine. It is forceful and clear—the voice of a girl who knows who she is. What will this girl do? The voice's power scares me and I don't waste any time skateboarding down the sidewalk, away from the playground and the pedestrian bridge.

When I get home, the whole family is in the living room, waiting for me.

"Angie, where were you? We were close to calling the police," Grandma says.

"I was skateboarding around the school."

"You can't just go for hours on end without telling us. We're responsible for you. You could have called us; you have a cell phone now."

"I left it here. Besides, Gramps knew I was going."

My grandfather drops his chin to his chest. I know then that although he has the love, he doesn't have the spine to cover for me.

"The woman next door told us that she had seen you go down the street on your skateboard."

Who? Oh, that lady next door, Mrs. O. "I don't like her," I say before thinking.

Grandma looks slightly pleased. "Why do you say that?" she asks.

I can feel the sweat balling up on my nose. "I don't like the way she looks at me."

"Now, An-jay, you don't even know her—" says Gramps.

"She does have that look," interrupts Grandma.

"Michi—"

"Well, anyway . . ." Grandma composes herself. "You can't be skateboarding in the street like that. You might get yourself run over."

I want to escape to somewhere. But there is no place to run to, except for the bathroom.

"Your dad called," Janet says as I walk toward the hallway.

I stop. "What did he say? Did he want me to call back?"

Janet shakes her head. "He said he'll call you."

"See, Angela?" Grandma says. "When you play around, you may miss something important."

# 9

# Tofu, Miso, and Nori

I move into my mother's old room the next day. Grandma Michi used the room as storage space for her crafts, as if the 1001-cranes room was not enough.

The Singer sewing machine, shaped like a horse saddle, is still in the room, pushed into the corner. But the bolts of fabric and the bags of yarn have been relocated.

There are a matching dresser and vanity set, along with the bed frame, made of pressed wood and painted white. The edges are scalloped, fake French, which is perhaps the worst kind of fake. My mother must have felt the same way, because she has trashed it with stickers of peace signs, the Budweiser man in a cape, a multicolored Peter Max cloud, and a bloodred STP oil logo.

I search the empty drawers of the vanity, trying to find any scraps of paper, any indication of who my mother was at my age. I discover a stack of blue ribbons for excellence in a number of talents—running, even gardening. Underneath the ribbons is something hard. A book—no, a diary. It has a cheap lock, and no key is to be found. I rip the flimsy flap that is supposed to ensure the privacy of the diary's contents.

It is one of those daily diaries; 1968 is written on the front page.

My fingers peel apart the pages. Blank. But then, on July 18, there is this sentence: *I went to the store today and saw him.*

Who is 'him'? I wonder. I leaf through all the other pages. Empty. So I've gone to the trouble of destroying Mom's diary lock for this single line?

On top of the vanity, stuck in the corners of the mirror, are a couple of faded photos. They're group shots of some Asian girls. I can spot my mother immediately, even though her hair is down to her butt, and her eyebrows are plucked severely in the form of upside-down Vs. She is laughing—they all are—and I wonder if that was the last time my mother felt carefree.

I unpack the clothes from my duffel bag and put them into the dresser drawers. It seems strange that my clothes are in the same place hers were when she was my age.

Half an hour later, I step outside. Janet is on the porch, three kittens of different colors around her feet. "Tofu," she says, pointing to the white one. "Miso," the brown. "Nori," the black.

"I didn't know you had cats." I sit next to Janet and pick up Nori. I like black cats.

"They're not mine. They're stray. Dad is allergic to them. And Mom doesn't like them."

She then kneels down and pulls out an old pie tin from the crawl space underneath the house. There are small bits of cat food smeared in it. "Shhh—it's our secret," Aunt Janet says.

I smile. I'm happy to hold on to a good secret for once.

"Look, Nori likes you." Aunt Janet points to the black cat, which has curled up in the crook of my arm.

"You know," Aunt Janet says, rubbing Miso's nose, "I think your dad will call you today."

I get a phone call at dinner. We are eating spaghetti with ground beef; Gramps has rice with his noodles.

I race to pick up the receiver. It's a familiar voice. My mother's.

"Hi, how's everything?" Her nose sounds stuffed up.

"Okay," I say. "What's wrong with your voice?"

"Allergies. Maybe it was from the smog down there." Mom tries to laugh, but it sounds fake.

"Where are you?"

"Home."

I wait to hear some signs that my dad is in the house as well. A television sportscast in the background, maybe the clanging of plates and pans in the kitchen. But nothing.

"Have you made any friends?" my mother asks.

"No," I say, trying to push the skateboarder's face

from my mind. "I've barely been here. Anyway, I'm surrounded by old people," I whisper.

"Now stop complaining. Have you gotten any customers yet?"

"No. I'm still trying to learn how to fold these things. Grandma Michi even grades my cranes."

That piece of news doesn't seem to faze my mother. "Well, if all goes well, Mom told me that she's going to give you half the money for every display you work on. A hundred and fifty dollars each. Some college kids don't even make that much for a week's worth of work."

My mother is good at distractions, but I'm not going to let her get away with it this time. "I haven't spoken to Dad yet. He has my cell phone number, doesn't he?"

Silence. "Angie." I can barely hear my mother's voice. She clears her throat. "Angie," she says again, more loudly. "Your father has moved out."

I feel as though I'm falling backward into a dark hole. The world is spinning. It shouldn't be a surprise, but it is. My nose starts to run. Somehow, this feels different from last time. Like this is going to be forever.

"Angie, are you there?"

"Yeah," I say. "Can I come back home now?"

"I need you to stay with Grandma and Gramps."

"For how long?"

"I'm not sure. There are some issues I'm dealing with."

"Issues? What kind of issues?"

"I can't say right now, Angie." Her tone gets flat; her momentary softness is gone.

I really start to cry now and Grandma gets up from the table and takes the phone from me.

"An-jay," Gramps calls, but I ignore him and run outside.

I hope to see the kittens wandering around. But they're gone. Instead, there's the next-door lady, Mrs. O, kneeling by her trash can.

I turn away for a moment and wipe my face with the front of my T-shirt. I know that I look awful. When I cry, my eyelids swell up. It probably wouldn't be a big deal if I had *hakujin* eyes, but I have Asian eyes. Slightly double eyelids that expand four times when wet with tears. Not a pretty sight.

I stare at Mrs. O for a minute and then gingerly walk toward her. I smell something putrid. Vomit. I can't make out much on the lawn, but spy a milky liquid on some blades of grass.

She finally notices that I am there, watching her.

"Oh," she says, mopping up tears with the backs of her hands. She is wearing a lot of mascara, so there are black smudges all over her face now.

I turn to get my grandparents, and I guess she reads my mind.

"Don't do that. I'm all right." She slowly gets up. "It must have been something I ate."

That doesn't make any sense. There are bathrooms for that.

"Hey, Mom, you okay?" A white woman comes out of the house. She has brown hair that is cut at her chin and she is wearing a dress and heels. She must be a little younger than my mother, but her fashion style makes her seem older.

"Yes, yes." Mrs. O wipes her face again and quickly makes introductions. "This is the Inuis' granddaughter. Angela, right? My daughter-in-law Sarah."

I am surprised that she has remembered my name, and before I know it, the old woman has quickly escaped back into the house, leaving me with the daughter-in-law.

"Ah, well—nice to meet you." Sarah sniffs and frowns. "What's that smell?"

"Some of the stray cats," I say. "They got sick, I guess."

The daughter-in-law sticks her tongue out; it is tiny and pink, like the kittens'. Then she retreats into her in-laws' house.

I don't know why I said what I said. I don't like this Mrs. O or her husband, Jack—wasn't that what I told both Gramps and Grandma? As I pull out Gramps and Grandma's garden hose and aim water at the offensive barf, I can't help imagining Mrs. O and me together, standing in the same muck as those cows in Kettleman City.

MICHI'S 1001-CRANES FOLDING TIP NO. 3:
Fold with a sense of purpose and confidence. If you hesitate, you will most likely end up with a broken line.

# 10

# The Great Gambaru

Tonight I go to bed early. Early-early, at eight o'clock.

I am sticky and my eyes are swollen, but I don't bother to take a bath, wash my face, or even brush my teeth. And no one tells me I have to. Either they feel sorry for me or they are afraid.

Around nine o'clock, somebody knocks on the door. I don't answer, but the door opens slowly. Gramps. He sits on the edge of the bed. I can tell that he's putting most of his weight on his feet and legs, because the bed hardly sags.

"You're going to be all right, An-jay," he says, and I start crying again. I don't know if it's because he said "all right" or his nickname for me. Or maybe it's a combination of both.

"Nothing is ever going to be right, Gramps." My eyes feel as big as clamshells. "She won't even tell me everything that's going on."

Gramps doesn't say anything for a while. He rests his hands on his legs as if he's deep in thought. "You know, I once felt that my world was falling apart."

I can't imagine Gramps ever feeling depressed or sad.

"I was a little older than you. I was hoping to go to college. But the war came and we had to move out of our house and be locked up in a camp. The schools were rotten in camp. I was mad. Real mad.

"Then my boss at the mess hall sat me down and had a talk with me. The first heart-to-heart talk I ever really had with a grown man. Even my own father never talked to me. Like my dad, my boss was from Japan and couldn't speak English that well. But one thing he taught me was *gambaru*."

"Gam-ba-roo?" I ask. It sounds like "kangaroo," and I almost start to laugh.

"Your parents never talked to you about *gambaru*?"

I shake my head.

" '*Gambaru*' means 'to persevere.' To hang in there. When everything looks bleak and rough, to charge ahead anyway." Gramps pauses and I hear a weird knocking sound from his mouth. I know that it's from his false teeth. When I was ten, I nearly died when I saw Gramps's dentures floating in a glass of water in the bathroom. I've since gotten used to it. Gramps is still Gramps even without his real teeth. "Do you know what I'm saying, An-jay?"

I don't answer. I don't even nod. I don't want to let

what he's saying soak in, because it would mean I would have to change. And that's the last thing I want to do.

He turns and pats the top of my head, the crazy hair that's sticking out on top of my pillow. There's the flower smell again. "You'll be all right. You're tough. You're like your mother, who's like your grandma."

I can't imagine that I'm anything like either of them.

"I know you feel that everything's been taken away from you. But you'll get things back. It just won't be quite like before. But it'll still be good. Now, you sleep."

# Dreaming Dad

When I wake up the next day, my eyelids are quadruple-size. King-size. Supersize. I look like I've been stung by a bunch of killer bees.

I go to the kitchen to get some ice cubes to reduce the swelling. Grandma's already there, washing some dishes.

"You now have your first one-thousand-and-one-cranes project," she tells me. She looks at me face to face and doesn't even acknowledge that my eyes are swollen shut. "Next door."

"They're married already."

"It's their wedding anniversary. Their fortieth. They came over this morning. Mrs. Oyama specifically asked for you to oversee the folding."

"Me?"

"They want the family to be involved. The two *haku-*

*jin* daughters-in-law will be folding the cranes. You'll be training them."

"Can't you just give them your booklet?"

Grandma doesn't say anything and puts a dried plate away. I know that if Gramps was around, he would comment, "They're *hakujin*. What do they know?"

"How about you? Aunt Janet?"

"I guess you made quite an impression on Mrs. Oyama." Grandma dries the prongs of a fork with her dish towel. "They've invited you for dinner tomorrow to discuss the particulars."

It is decided. I can't argue. I spend the rest of the day icing my eyes and reading a manga that I brought with me. Nobody bothers me. Aunt Janet makes me a peanut butter and jelly sandwich, covers it with a napkin, and leaves it on the dining room table.

Tonight my father calls my cell phone. I know it's him even before I answer. I look at the digital screen, and sure enough, it says DAD'S CELL.

When I hear Dad's voice, I feel not sad, but angry.

I let him stumble around trying to put awkward words together.

Finally, I whisper, "Why?"

"What, Angie? I can't hear you."

"Why didn't you tell me when I left? I knew about the apartment. Your new landlady called."

Silence. "That was wrong of me," Dad says. "We

should have talked it over before you left. I just didn't want to make it harder for you to go to L.A."

No, you didn't want to make it harder for yourself, I think. "Why are you doing this?"

"Honey, it's not anything I'm doing against you. Sometimes these things happen. This is between your mother and me. You never think something like this is going to happen. But things change; people change."

"Was Mom nicer before?"

Dad then laughs. "No, she was the same *monku* girl the day I met her." I can't help smiling a little myself.

"Where are you living, Dad?"

"I'm in an apartment, just down the street."

"How many bedrooms?"

"Well, it's a studio. So I guess it's zero bedrooms."

I imagine Dad in his sweats, surrounded by brown boxes in his one-room apartment.

"You'll be able to visit me anytime."

"Can I come now? I won't be any trouble. I can sleep in a sleeping bag, even."

Dad is silent for a minute. "No. No, right now, it's better if you're with your grandparents."

"How about Jii-chan and Baa-chan?" At least I would be closer to my house.

"No," says Dad in his no-*monku* voice. "It'll be better if you stay put. At least for now."

So is this really it? The end of us? I want to fix it, to be the glue that fastens my parents together again. My heart starts to race. I try to say something but only manage a squeak.

"I know that you don't understand, Angie, but none of this—none of it is your fault."

I feel tears come to my eyes; I have a limitless supply of them. I wish tears were finite, like the water in a water bottle. I would be all dried up by now. "I don't want to be alone, Daddy," I finally say.

"You'll never be alone, honey. You'll always have me and your mother. And Jii-chan and Baa-chan, Grandma Michi and Gramps, Aunt Janet. We'll always, always be there for you."

I swallow a lump of air in my throat. When you swallow a cry like that, it feels good, at least in the short run.

I don't hear what my dad says next. My dad is a dreamer. He dreams about buildings that don't exist. He just imagines beams, walls, and roofs. He draws them from his mind. Other people do the messy work. I know because I've been on a construction site before. I've worn those funny hard hats and followed my dad over dirt and gravel. One time I overheard one construction worker say to another, "He's crazy. It may work on a blueprint, but not in reality." The other merely shrugged. He obviously agreed but didn't care enough to voice his doubts.

"So what are your plans for tomorrow?" Dad asks.

"Not much," I say. "Have to go next door for dinner." I'm not looking forward to it, but I try to hold on to Gramps's word: *gambaru.*

# No More Spam

As I sit at the Oyama family's table the next evening, I wish for a moment that I was staying here instead of at my grandparents'. For one thing, all the furnishings have clean lines—no fancy scalloped edges or extras. I feel that my mind can relax; I don't have to tie myself into knots to deflect all the physical chaos around me like at Grandma Michi's house.

The other thing is the food. Instead of Spam with rice, spaghetti with a side of rice, or chili on rice, dinner is a salad with fresh tomatoes and bits of basil, straight from the garden, and chicken fajitas, steaming with fat slices of green pepper, onion, and tomato. Not one grain of rice in sight.

I'm a bottomless pit. My face doesn't leave my plate. I keep scooping food into my mouth, my head down so I don't have to join in their conversation, which is extremely fake polite—you know: the kind that dances like bubbles floating in the air and then pops into nothingness.

While they eat, they don't watch cable news and call politicians idiots, like my mother sometimes does. And they don't make comments about their neighbors or cutting remarks about white people. Of course, that really wouldn't make any sense here.

There are six Oyamas around the rosewood dining table—Mrs. O, Mr. O, their two sons, and their white daughters-in-law. The two sons, Jack Jr. and Arthur, the younger one, are both engineers at different companies; Grandma Michi filled me in on that.

It has taken me a long time to understand what engineers do, and to be honest, I'm still not absolutely clear. When I was in elementary school, I always pictured an engineer wearing striped overalls, a puffy hat, and a red scarf around his neck and standing inside a locomotive. Emilie, whose father is an engineer, corrected me. She said that engineers sit at desks and design machines, work similar to an architect's, only with moving parts. Driving a train seems so much more exciting.

Anyway, both of Mrs. O's sons have the same kind of job. They even have similar short haircuts, although Jack Jr.'s hair is parted on the right; Arthur's, the left. Neither is bad-looking for being kind of old, I guess. I mean, they're not ugly, for sure. I like Arthur's look a little better. He has thick, shaggy eyebrows like his father's. He is a little less manicured, a little wild around the edges. Jack Jr., on the other hand, looks shiny and smooth, like someone scrubs him down every night.

Jack Jr.'s wife is Sarah, the woman I met outside the house; Arthur's is Helen. Helen is a typical freckle-faced redhead, freckles on every exposed part of her body, from her eyelids to her earlobes. I love redheads and had a crush on one in my school in Mill Valley. He didn't have the same feelings for Asian girls, I guess.

"Angela's a pretty name," Helen says, using that high-pitched voice adults reserve for children.

I'm in a bad mood and want just to concentrate on my food. "My parents named me after Angela Davis," I say.

Helen then exchanges glances with her husband, and Sarah with hers. Obviously the Oyamas can't relate to a former Black Panther who was on the FBI's Ten Most Wanted List about the time I was born.

Mr. O seems to feel like he needs to dig into my background more. "What do your parents do?"

"My dad's an architect. My mom is a lawyer. Just part-time."

"So, not doing so bad for former radicals." Mr. O smiles.

"My dad went to the Green Party convention last year. I walked the precinct with him." I like the word "precinct." It sounds very criminal.

Silence again. "The fajitas are good, Mom," says Helen.

"Yes, real tender," Sarah echoes.

All through the conversation, Mrs. O is quiet. I notice that she doesn't eat much on her plate. She sits across the table from me and just stares. Everyone here seems to notice that I have somehow placed a spell on Mrs. O, and because of that, they are no doubt going to watch me very closely.

# 13

# Dueling Daughters-in-law

After dinner, the men retreat to the living room for a baseball game on TV while the women take the dishes and the glasses to the kitchen. I stay in my chair, not quite sure where I belong.

"No, no, I got it," Mrs. O says, shooing her daughters-in-law back into the living room. "You all have to start on our anniversary project." She then nods at me, and I know that that is my cue to get the folding lessons started.

Grandma Michi has given me a fishing-tackle box filled with supplies. I take out two of her booklets and give one to each daughter-in-law.

"I better go wash my hands," Sarah says after reading Michi's Tip Number 1.

"I think my hands are clean enough." Helen squeezes her freckled hands and smiles faintly at me.

When Sarah returns to the table, I notice that there

is a coolness between the two women. They never seem to address each other directly and they keep their gazes on me.

Sarah is better at folding. It is obvious that she is good at following directions. "I did it." She waves a completed crane and it is undeniable: she has scored an A on her first try.

Helen, on the other hand, struggles. You can see the white in all her folds, and when she's done, the resulting paper structure looks more like a crushed Dixie cup than a bird.

Mrs. O returns to the table to do some folding of her own. Her face is a bit greenish but her daughters-in-law are concentrating so hard on the origami that they don't seem to notice.

The next hour and a half passes with more of the same. Sarah is like a machine; she produces one perfect crane after another. Helen, between sighs, folds one damaged, balled-up crane after another. I can just see Grandma Michi shaking her head. *We can't use those. Unacceptable.* Mrs. O, meanwhile, sits for a few minutes, breathes in the scene at the table, and then goes away somewhere else—maybe outside by the trash can again?

It's late, so I divide a stack of wrapped origami paper into two piles. Four hundred sheets for one daughter-in-law, and another four hundred for the other.

"How can I make four hundred cranes on my own?" The high pitch of Helen's voice hurts my ears. As if responding to a dog whistle, Arthur comes to her side.

"What's going on?" he asks.

"It's too much. I can't do this. I never was good at crafty things."

I totally understand how Helen feels, but she's making a big deal out of nothing. So she's bad at folding cranes—join the club. At least she doesn't have Grandma Michi grading her work. Meanwhile, Sarah has her dozens of perfect A-grade cranes lined up in front of her like military jets ready to take off. Her husband is now standing in back of her chair, and I can easily read the look on his face: *My wife's are better than your wife's.*

"My parents could hire you to do these, right? Fold all the cranes?" Arthur says.

I nod. I am feeling a little overwhelmed, thinking about all the cranes I will have to fold.

Mrs. O returns to the table, and Arthur pitches his idea to her. "Mom, why don't you have the Inuis handle the whole thing? Helen is busy with work, and so is Sarah—"

"I don't mind," Sarah interrupts.

"Well, anyway, most everyone is busy, so why don't you let Angela do all the folding?"

This is obviously not what Mrs. O had in mind. "We're supposed to work on these together. Like a quilt." Mrs. O's voice is steady and clear.

"Is that what this whole thing is about? Louise Takeyama's family quilt?"

Mrs. O frowns.

"I saw it," Arthur says. "It was on display at church last Sunday, right? So, is this again about how we can keep up with the Takeyamas?"

Mrs. O's mouth quivers. She has lines around her lips, like my grandmother, but instead of being straight and defined, they are broken and dotted. "Excuse me," she says, leaving the table again.

With Mrs. O's exit comes the entrance of her husband. Even though he hasn't been in the room until now, he knows everything that has been going on. "This isn't about Louise Takeyama or anyone else. This is our anniversary, and you'll make this for us. For me and your mother." Jack Sr.'s voice takes on a serious and deep tone, a heavy blanket falling over all of us.

At this point I figure out that the whole project really has nothing to do with the 1001 cranes or even the anniversary celebration. And that they have brought me in because they believed I wouldn't understand what was going on below the surface. And they were right; I don't. But I can feel that something is wrong. I'm supersensitive right now anyway; I can smell even a whiff of conflict.

Jack Sr. keeps talking. "So I don't want to hear any more of it. No more *monku*."

My dad's special word. I look up, surprised. Jack Jr. must think I need a translation. His lips have been pressed together and he finally says, "Whining. My dad is sick of whining. And I am, too."

His words burn in my ears, and I know that Helen

must be feeling it as well. She blinks rapidly, freckles on her eyelids appearing and disappearing.

"You're such a jerk," Arthur shoots back at his older brother. I then close the tackle box. I know that our first 1001-cranes folding session is over.

I pack my things and then notice that I'm alone at the table. I don't see Helen or Arthur. Jack Jr. and Sarah, deep in conversation, are huddled on the couch in the living room.

I look down a hallway, where the bathroom is. The back bedroom is lit and the door is open. Mr. O is massaging Mrs. O's shoulders. Her chin is down on her chest. "Oh, that's where it's sore, Jack," she says.

"Mom, you can't overdo it, okay?"

I know that Mr. O's calling her Mom doesn't mean he thinks Mrs. O is his mother. Gramps does the same thing, only he sometimes yells out "Grandma" when he wants Grandma Michi's attention.

"Oooh, there, there. That's it," Mrs. O says.

I stand and watch them for another minute. Somehow, seeing Mr. O massage Mrs. O makes me feel better.

Once I'm at my grandparents' house, Grandma peppers me with questions. "So, what did it look like inside?"

"Michi—" Gramps says.

"After all these years, they never let me in. Just keep me standing in the doorway," Grandma says.

"It looked normal," I say. Normal like us in Mill Valley, but maybe not Inui normal. I don't mention anything about the tension between the two brothers and their wives. Grandma Michi would relish it, I'm sure. But for some reason I remain protective of Mrs. O. "Mrs. Oyama wants me to come back every Friday night. Have dinner with them and then help the daughters-in-law fold."

"Is she a good cook?"

"Of course she's a good cook," Gramps says. "Remember that casserole she brought when you had your gallbladder surgery?"

"It tasted different. Had eggplant and zucchini in it," Janet remarks, as if there's no other vegetable than iceberg lettuce.

"She had a cancer before," Grandma says.

"They thought she was going to die," Aunt Janet adds.

"I think she had both breasts removed."

I start to feel a little sick to my stomach and tug my bra through my T-shirt.

"Miracle she's survived this long," Gramps adds.

"Well, cancer survivor or no cancer survivor," Grandma declares, "if Ruth Oyama wants to take so much of my granddaughter's time, she'll have to pay extra."

# 14

# Crazy Kawaguchi

Gramps says that in business, when it rains, it pours. Sure enough, the next day another customer, in a suit, nylons, heels, and pearls, walks through the door of the flower shop. She tells us that her name is Lisa Kawaguchi. She comes with a bunch of extras, including a large leather Day-Timer and an assortment of high-tech gadgets.

"I heard that you also do one-thousand-and-one-cranes displays," she says.

Grandma Michi gives her a once-over before speaking. She looks as if she can sense that this woman will be trouble. "Yes," she says, and, probably against her better judgment, pulls out the 1001-cranes book.

After glancing at every plastic-covered page in our album, the woman seems satisfied. She introduces herself, pronouncing her last name "Ka-wa-GOO-chi," like she's a hungry grizzly bear on a food hunt. At that moment, to me she becomes Kawaguchi rather than Lisa.

She opens her Day-Timer to the back, releases the three metal rings to present a photocopied picture to Grandma. It is of a line of old men in black kimonos. She taps the circular design on the shoulders of their clothing. Aunt Janet told me that Japanese families wore their crests on their funeral attire. "This is my mother's *mon*." It is simple. A six-point star that resembles a pin I used to put on my Brownie sash.

"Fine. We can do that." Grandma doesn't waste any time and tells her how much it's going to cost. Maybe she wants to scare off Kawaguchi.

"But the design is simple."

But Grandma doesn't seem like she's going to budge.

They go back and forth and then Kawaguchi notices Gramps's flower arrangements. She's impressed, looks through our wedding flowers book, and says she'll also order a bridal bouquet and boutonnieres if Grandma gives her a break.

The two women nod and the deal is struck.

"I'd like a drawing of the display. Maybe on graph paper. And I'd like you to prepare a swatch."

"Swatch?"

"I just want to see how the cranes will look together. And I want it in silver. You can fax or e-mail me the drawing this weekend."

"We don't have a fax. And I don't e-mail."

Kawaguchi puckers her lips. She wears a tangerine

lipstick that doesn't seem to smear no matter how she contorts her mouth. She presses buttons on a digital device and then flips her Day-Timer past rows and columns highlighted in neon pink, yellow, and blue. Kawaguchi's life is neatly categorized, stacked, and color coded.

"Well, I'll be meeting the wedding coordinator at the Gardena Buddhist Temple on Monday. I won't have time to come by here. Can you meet me there?"

This is a test of wills; I can just feel it. "My granddaughter, Angela, can deliver it. It's walking distance from here."

What? I think. I don't mind being sent out from the shop, but I don't want to deal with Kawaguchi on my own.

Kawaguchi gives me a look. I know that she doesn't think much of me. I don't care, because the same goes for me about her. "I guess that will be all right," she finally says. "Two o'clock on Monday. I'll be in the sanctuary."

She then slaps her date book shut, as if warning me that there will be repercussions if I don't show.

# 15

# Wet Carnations

The next few days are filled with folding, folding, and more folding. Origami cranes as big as the Dumbos on the Disneyland ride even show up in my dreams. They fly past my head one after another. When I wake up, my fingers are moving above me, folding invisible cranes.

Gramps has told me that during dark times, it's good to keep your mind on other things. I think that's definitely true for Grandma Michi, because she's constantly moving. She doesn't watch much TV or many movies, and when she does, she's either knitting or clipping coupons. She doesn't talk about her dark times, but she wears them on her face sometimes when she doesn't think people are looking.

Origami is my medicine for right now. The cranes are my distractions and I'm grateful for them. Now most of them go into the A pile, or at least the B pile. I make Cs when I start thinking about Mom and Dad.

Mom and Dad take turns calling me, so I figure that they talked to make sure at least one of them would touch base with me every day.

On Sunday afternoon I try not to think about the skateboarders—well, one certain skateboarder—at the middle school. He probably forgot about me, I figure.

On Monday morning I get up early to go to the flower market with Gramps. He goes to the flower market three times a week. He tells me that they are actually two flower markets that stand opposite each other in downtown Los Angeles, but most people think they're just one. The one on the west side of Wall Street is the "American" market, and the one on the east is "Japanese." We go into the Japanese one.

When I first heard of the flower market, I thought of a book I had read that took place in England during Victorian times. There was a drawing of an open-air market, with women with big breasts, wearing gauzy peasant dresses and flower wreaths in their hair, carrying baskets of daisies and roses. But the reality is completely different. The flower market is encased in concrete, surrounded by tents and refrigerator boxes where homeless men and women live, and run-down diners. We park our van in a paved lot and Gramps borrows a flat cart on rollers from a black man named Johnny. Johnny seems to be a good friend of Gramps's. "You have a mighty pretty granddaughter there," he says, and he looks at me hard, as if he means it.

Gramps seems to know everyone who works in the

flower market. We go down in the elevator to a big open area filled with plastic containers of every kind of flower you can think of. There are stands throughout the room and Gramps tells me that he has "standing orders" with the best growers and wholesalers. At least half of the workers here are Japanese and have funny names like Jibo, Mamo, Itch, Taxie, Haruo, and Froggy. They smile at me and offer me flower bouquets wrapped in newspaper. "Next time you come, we'll buy you some breakfast at the coffee shop," they tell me.

"I like the flower market," I tell him on the way home. His van is full of buckets sloshing with water and blooms.

"What's not to like?"

When we arrive at the flower shop, somebody all dressed in white is sitting at the front door. The girl, Rachel Joseph. She gets up immediately when she sees Gramps's van, but her face falls when she realizes it's me, not Grandma Michi, in the passenger seat.

Gramps parks in the back, next to the tool shack, and starts to unload the flowers from the van. Rachel rounds the back corner of the shop.

"Where's Auntie Michi?"

Since Gramps doesn't acknowledge her, I feel that I have to say something. "She's at home working on a last-minute display," I say. I figure that she will leave now, but she remains in front of me, pulling at her orange belt.

"Well, do you know when she'll be coming back?"

Oh my God, what a pest. Emilie complains about her little sister and brother, but I never took her that seriously before. I shrug, thinking that now Rachel will go for sure, but instead, she runs to the back of the open van, picks up a plastic container full of pink carnations, and begins to follow Gramps into the shop.

"Hey." I pull at the container. The water sloshes and drips onto my Vans. "You're not supposed to do that."

Rachel has opened the back screen door and positions one leg inside the shop, one leg outside on the welcome mat. I don't know what an orange belt means, but I have to admit that she's strong for her size. "I help Uncle Nick all the time," she says. Her grip remains strong around the container's handle.

Now, I don't know why, but this little girl is making me mad. This is my Gramps. My Grandma Michi. Not hers. I know it sounds stupid—I mean, I'm old enough to know better and I'm not sure how much I even like my grandmother—but I feel that I have to fight or I won't have anything left anymore.

"Leave it."

"No."

"I'll take it."

"No."

My fingers are getting red from tugging so hard on the container's handle. "I'm not kidding," I warn her.

"Me either."

"Listen, why don't you go back to your *own* family?"

Something I've said works, and Rachel releases her

grip. The container falls onto the welcome mat, soaking it and part of Rachel's *gi*. The screen door snaps closed, breaking the stems of the carnations.

"See? See what you've done!"

Rachel's brown eyes are filled with tears. First I think she's just mad or spiteful. But I soon realize that she's scared.

I feel totally bad now. And ashamed. Before I can say anything else, Rachel has run out of the parking lot.

"What happened here?" Gramps asks.

"Uh—I—"

Gramps kneels down and picks up the heads of the broken carnations. "Ah, not to worry. I can use these for the boutonnieres for the Lopez wedding."

# 16

# Tony

After we unload, I go back inside the shop and try not to think of Rachel Joseph. I mean, she was just getting in the way, right? She didn't have any business being at the flower shop. Grandma said that I should be nice to her, but I wasn't that mean to her, was I?

I eat a bologna sandwich at the shop counter. I fold probably twenty C cranes before Gramps reminds me to get ready to walk to the Buddhist temple. Grandma has drawn a map for me, plus I skateboarded there that one time, so I know exactly where it is. I want to take my skateboard this time, too, but Gramps says it's a bit un-professional. Besides, he tells me, I have to carry the sample design, all plotted out on graph paper, and the swatch of glued cranes.

He puts those items into a manila envelope for me and I wave to him before I leave.

I turn the corner at the liquor store, and a skateboarder squeals to a stop, almost crashing into the left side of my body. I don't know if it's because he surprises me or because it's *him*—yes, the guy from the schoolyard—but I loosen my grip on the manila envelope. It slips through my hand, down a hole by the curb, and into the gutter.

"No, no!" I scream loudly, and I almost don't even care that I'm embarrassing myself in front of *him.*

The boy obviously has fast reflexes, because before I'm finished screaming, he's down on the pavement, his cheek pressed against the ground, to try to retrieve my package for Kawaguchi. He desperately waves his hand toward the sad manila envelope, which is soaked in gunk and surrounded by trash in the gutter. But his arm is not long enough.

I cover my face. "I can't believe it. What am I going to tell Gramps?" I say, but I'm really wondering what I'm going to tell Grandma Michi.

"What's in there?" The boy stands and brushes dirt from his jeans. He misses something dark on his left cheek, but I say nothing about that.

"Oh." I sit against the wall of the liquor store building. "It's really hard to explain."

"I have time," he says, kneeling down beside me.

"I make these cranes," I say.

"You mean the origami kind?"

"You know about them?"

"I've made some before."

It seems that the boy can easily read my face. "Boys

can do origami, too." He smiles and I notice that one side of his mouth goes up a little higher than the other.

"Anyway, my grandparents have a business to sell these one-thousand-and-one-cranes displays for weddings and things like that. That's why I'm here—to help them."

"That's cool. So that's origami down there." The boy points to the gutter.

I nod. "It was a sample, only about twenty silver cranes. And a diagram of the design on graph paper. I'm supposed to meet her—" I fish my cell phone out of my pocket. "Crap. In ten minutes."

"Just call your grandparents. Tell them what happened."

"You don't know my grandma. She's going to be pissed. She's going to tell my mom, and my mom's going to be pissed. Everyone's pissed right now. My mom hates my dad, my dad's left, and everything's all messed up." I don't mention anything about yelling at Rachel Joseph, but that's on my mind, too. Everything comes out so fast I don't realize that I've violated my family's rule about not sharing secrets with outsiders.

"That sucks," he says. And for some reason, those two simple words make me start to cry. *I'm really not a crybaby,* I want to tell him. But the fact that I'm crying will make that sound stupid. My nose starts to run and I'm horrified. I wipe away my snot with the side of my index finger, but there's still more, like lines of a spiderweb.

"Here," he says, pulling his sleeve toward me. "Use this."

"I don't want to mess up your shirt."

"Use it. I've had worse things on my clothes."

I duck my head toward his arm. His skin is nice and tan, like a perfectly roasted marshmallow. I gingerly take the bottom of his sleeve and lightly brush the tip of my nose with it. His sleeve smells like burnt leaves and sweat. I like the scent.

"Thanks," I say, and I mean it. Not just anyone would let a perfect stranger wipe her nose on his clothes. "Now what am I going to do?"

He gets up and offers his hand to me. He helps me stand and says, "I'm Tony, by the way."

"I'm Angie," I say back.

"I know." He smiles again. "I think I can help you." He leads me around the corner and into the liquor store I stopped at a couple of Sundays ago to buy gummy worms. He waves to the elderly man behind the counter. "That's my uncle Carlos," he explains, leading me past rows of potato chips and refrigerated drinks.

We go into a back room that's dark and musty-smelling. He tells me to sit down at a Formica table and then he leaves for a moment. He returns with a package of graph paper and a roll of aluminum foil.

"Do you think you can remember what that design looks like?" he asks.

Tony says that he loves to draw and wants to be a cartoonist someday. I tell him that I want to be a writer of manga books, and he jokes that we should collaborate. I draw the star on one corner of the graph paper and he works fast to replicate it on the entire sheet. Meanwhile, I'm supposed to fold cranes with squares of aluminum foil. It's not going to work that well, but I do so anyway.

I don't even check the time because we're working as fast as we can. Before we know it, we're finished. I've taped the malformed cranes to a piece of cardboard and he has graphed Kawaguchi's family crest. I'm surprised, because his drawing looks almost as good as Aunt Janet's. For a moment I think that I can pull it off.

Tony borrows his uncle's bicycle, an old three-speed with a dorky basket on the front of it. Before we leave, I tell him about the dirt on his face. "You have something here," I say, pointing to my cheek.

He rubs his face but he misses. "Where?"

I brush the dirt away with the tips of my fingers. His face feels warm, like he's been out in the sun.

He holds the bicycle still so I can sit on the handles with my thighs hanging over the basket. Tony has put our designs in a backpack for safekeeping. When we arrive at the Buddhist temple, he steadies the bicycle so I can get off. He's strong, much stronger than he looks. He unzips his backpack and it smells like cigarette smoke. He then hands me the crane-taped cardboard and the graph paper.

"Thanks," I say. I cannot believe how nice he's been.

"Do you want me to come in with you?"

I shake my head. There's already enough explaining I have to do. How would I explain Tony?

"Come to the school this Sunday." He presses down on my wrist, and my arm begins to tingle.

I make no promises, but I know that nothing will keep me away from him on Sunday.

MICHI'S 1001-CRANES FOLDING TIP NO. 4:
Be careful about the edges and the corners
of your origami. Those are the places that
are the most visible.

# Broken *Butsudan*

For some reason, when I'm nervous or doing PE, I don't sweat where most people do. All my sweat goes through my body and lands on my nose and my upper lip. Like right now in front of the Buddhist temple. Salty drips run down the middle of my face onto my T-shirt. I know that they are salty because some of my sweat lands on my lips and goes into my mouth.

I hesitate a moment in front of the gate and then open it before running up the concrete stairs. Once I reach the temple building, I almost crash into a man wearing a polo shirt and shorts.

"Sorry, sorry," I tell him. He's Japanese American, with skinny eyes and big, thick tree-trunk arms. "I need to find Mrs.—I mean Ms. Kawaguchi. She has a meeting here."

"You look like you've been running in a 5K." The

man laughs. "I don't think she's here yet, but you can wait for her in the sanctuary."

I beat Kawaguchi? I could have spent more time gluing the cranes! There isn't anything I can do about it now, though.

I walk down a hallway with the man.

"Are you her niece?"

"Oh, no," I say, maybe a little too emphatically. I made it sound like being her niece would be horrible. Well, actually, it might. But I wasn't trying to make Kawaguchi out to be evil. Really.

"I'm here to deliver this."

The man frowns at the wilted cardboard and the taped aluminum foil origami cranes.

"I know that it looks kind of bad. Had an accident." Maybe it's all Tony's fault, but words begin to spill out of my mouth again, like sludge from a sewer pipe. The man listens as I tell him about Kawaguchi, the envelope in the sewer, and how Grandma Michi doesn't think I can do much right.

"So Ms. Kawaguchi is a tough customer?"

"She's kind of mean," I whisper. I'm surprised that I've said such a thing to a stranger but it just came out.

"Just go through that door." He gestures to a narrow hallway.

I speed up the stairs into a giant hall. No one is in there, only empty rows of wooden pews and a huge altar in front of the room, which smells of incense. The altar looks like a giant black wardrobe open to reveal shiny gold ornaments and Japanese writing. I've seen this kind of altar before. I know that it's called a *butsudan*.

When Jii-chan's brother, Uncle Tai, died, the family had the funeral in a Buddhist church on the other side of San Francisco Bay. I hadn't known Uncle Tai that well. I'd seen him only once a year, at Thanksgiving. There was no coffin at his funeral. Only an old picture of him in a fancy frame. We had to go up in front of the *butsudan*, where there were containers of incense that looked like ash, and sprinkle that incense into a larger pot of burning incense. My mother told me that I should bow before and after I did the incense thing, but I forgot. I hoped that no one was watching me.

It turned out that Uncle Tai's wife, Auntie Momo, was staring at me from the front pew. She looked so sad, and when I passed by, she clutched at my elbow as if she was trying to cheer me up. I felt bad, because I couldn't remember much about Uncle Tai. He'd sat on a couch with the other old people and eaten his Thanksgiving turkey on a TV tray in the back room of the house my dad had grown up in. I don't think I ever really had a conversation with him, other than nodding when he asked me if I was doing okay at school.

I start to feel like I have to pee, or go *shi-shi*, as Gramps calls it. But I hold it in. I'm glad that I've stayed, because a few minutes later Kawaguchi enters, wearing a new suit and the same pearls. Holding on to her Day-Timer, she's frowning. I bet she's the crabbiest bride around.

"Where's the wedding coordinator?" she asks me.

I shrug. I don't know if she's talking about the man who brought me to the sanctuary.

"What's that?" She points to my aluminum-foil cranes.

I reluctantly hand over Tony's drawing and the taped cranes.

"What is this made of? Tinfoil?"

More sweat drips from my nose to the tile floor. I feel like my body is getting swirled up into a dark tornado.

Before anything more happens, an older woman with a pad of paper appears from the back door. "Hello, Ms. Kawaguchi," she says, and I instantly know that I'm safe. At least for a few more minutes.

*You wait,* Kawaguchi mouths, and I sink into one of the front pews.

"I'm so sorry to keep you waiting. Your fiancé couldn't make it?"

"He's in Europe right now. On a business trip."

"Well, how wonderful. Unfortunately, I have a piece of bad news to report. Our minister is having health problems."

The color seems to be draining from Kawaguchi's face. "Health problems?"

"Yes, a stroke."

"This is awful. This is just awful." Kawaguchi hugs her Day-Timer to her chest as if she's trying to console it.

The wedding coordinator nods. "I know it's just such a shock, but I'm sure Sensei will recover."

"By my wedding date?"

The coordinator's mouth falls into a straight line. Even I know that it is pretty low-class to say something like that when somebody's sick.

"It's just that my parents got married by Reverend Nako," Kawaguchi says, trying to explain herself. "It would have been so perfect. We were even going to tell the photographer to pose us with the minister in the same exact way."

"We've already been assigned an interim minister. I think he knows you, in fact. He mentioned something about you two going to the same college."

Kawaguchi looks confused. "Same college . . . What's his name?"

The back door opens, and it's the man who served as my tour guide. "Hello, Lisa. It's been a long time."

Kawaguchi is surprised and spills her Day-Timer on the floor. The rings of her binder spring open and the pages fly out, littering the front of the sanctuary with a rainbow of dates and lists of things to do. The other woman immediately kneels down to collect all the loose pages.

Oh my God, I think. This guy, the minister, knows Kawaguchi. And I told the minister that Kawaguchi was mean. She's not going to be happy to hear that.

"You're the new minister here? I thought that you were out in Watsonville," Kawaguchi says.

"Been reassigned. It's so good to see you, Lisa. You look great."

Something in the way he looks at her makes me think that these two are more than college friends. Maybe the wedding coordinator gets the same impression, because she quickly excuses herself after giving Kawaguchi her Day-Timer pages.

Kawaguchi seems to forget that I'm in the sanctuary. That doesn't surprise me, because I'm pretty invisible most of the time. It's not necessarily a bad thing; sometimes it helps me figure out what's really going on.

"So you're the new minister here. For good?"

"Well, until Nako-sensei recuperates. Maybe some months."

"This isn't going to work, you know. Kevin is not going to like it."

"Is that his name: Kevin? What's his last? Maybe I know him."

"You don't know him. He doesn't need to know anything about you."

"Then why is it a problem that I conduct the ceremony?"

"You know what the problem is!"

"No, I don't."

"He's going to know. He'll sense it."

"What, is he a mind reader or something?"

"No, but he'll be able to tell. You can't do the ceremony. I'll just have to get another minister."

"Well, then you'll have to find another church."

"What are you talking about?"

"Lisa, churches aren't like hotel rooms. You can't just

pay money for the rental of the sanctuary. If you want this church, then I come with it. It's a package deal. I'm over you, if that's what you're worried about. I'm totally cool with doing your wedding."

"I'm not going to be able to find a temple on such short notice. And all the invitations are out already. I can't just change the location."

"Well, then, I guess you're stuck with me. We can be friends, Lisa."

"I don't need a friend right now. Just a minister."

Kawaguchi is so mean that I can't believe it. I start coughing and Kawaguchi finally notices me sitting in the pew.

"Oh, that's my new friend," the minister says.

I lower my head, hoping that I somehow won't be that visible. But it's too late.

"She tells me that she's doing some work for you." My fingers dig into my thighs. I cringe while waiting to hear him repeat how I described Kawaguchi: "kind of mean" or something like that. "She said that you were so easy to work for."

Kawaguchi is taken aback by that, maybe even more than I am. "Well, don't want to keep you here," she says to me. "Don't want your grandparents to worry."

"The deposit?" My voice is a mere squeak.

Kawaguchi digs in her purse and pulls out her checkbook. "Inui Flowers. A hundred and fifty dollars, right?"

# 18

# Ding-dong

On my way home I stop by Tony's uncle's store. The uncle—I think his name is Carlos—smiles down at me from behind the counter. He recognizes me and I feel special.

"Is Tony here?" I ask.

Uncle Carlos shakes his head. Using a page of an old receipt book, he writes down a number. Although it's summertime, he's wearing long sleeves, and the cuffs go down to his palms.

"You call him," he says to me, handing me the sheet from the receipt book.

I try to call Gramps and Grandma Michi first, but I get a busy signal. I try Tony's next, but I get his voice mail. "Thanks," I say. "It all worked out. This is Angie, by the way." I close the phone and feel silly, but a good silly. I have a check for Gramps and Grandma Michi in my back pocket. And Tony's phone number is now the fourth one to be entered into my cell phone.

Before I can open my grandparents' screen door, Grandma Michi beats me to it from the other side. I'm still smiling, but Grandma's not.

"What did you do to Rachel?" Her chin is stiff and her spotted neck is tight, like that of a lizard who's ready to slurp up an insect.

For a minute I forget who Rachel is.

"She went crying to her father. Her *gi* was sopping wet."

"She did that to herself, not me."

"But you said something to her, didn't you? She wouldn't say to her father, but he figured out that something you said hurt her feelings."

"I barely said anything to her. She was just getting in the way."

Grandma's eyes are like hammered-down nails. She doesn't blink. Not even once.

"I just told her to go back to her own family," I finally admit.

For a second I think that Grandma Michi is going to slap my face. Not that she has her hand out, but I notice that her fingers are rolled up like bear claw donuts.

"I want you to call and apologize to her."

"Why?" I say. "She was the one who was spilling water all over the place." My cheeks feel flushed like they do whenever I stretch the truth. The last thing I want to do is say I'm sorry to Rachel Joseph. But deep down inside, I know I did wrong.

The doorbell rings, and Grandma hesitates, as if she doesn't plan on answering it. She gets on her tippy-toes and looks through the eyehole. "What does *she* want?" I hear Grandma Michi mutter. She then opens the door with a big fake smile on her face.

It's the lady from next door, Mrs. O, and she wants to talk to me.

"I'd like to invite you to church with me. Mr. Oyama will be on a fishing trip, so I'll be on my own."

"Isn't that on Sunday?" I ask.

"Of course. It's always on Sunday."

I'm supposed to meet Tony on Sunday. That's the only thing on my mind.

"I don't think that I can make it," I tell her.

Grandma Michi then butts in from behind me. "She'll go," she says.

A few minutes later I'm using the poison red cell phone to talk to Mom. "Grandma Michi is making me go to church tomorrow."

"What kind of church?"

"A Christian church."

"Let me talk to Grandma."

I walk over to Grandma and hand the phone to her. She says a few words and then walks into her bedroom and closes the door.

I don't go try to overhear Grandma's one-way conversation with my mom. I pretty much know what she's telling her. After about ten minutes, Grandma comes out and shoves the phone back into my hand.

"Angela," Mom says, "I know that you're going through a lot right now. Maybe it's good if you go and meet some other girls your own age."

# 19

# Well Woman

It's not that I'm totally clueless about religion. My friend Abby goes to temple at certain times of the year, and instead of a Christmas tree, her family puts out a giant wooden star that they hang ornaments on. Instead of Santa Clauses or snowmen, tops called dreidels appear on tables in their living room. And I've been to Buddhist temples, like I mentioned before. And not only for funerals and New Year's rice cakes. Every summer Jii-chan and Baa-chan take me to an *Obon*, which is kind of a Japanese day of the dead.

But I've never been to Buddhist Sunday school or anything like that. It seems boring. I mean, we have to sit at desks five days a week for regular school. Why would I want to do that during the weekend, when I could be skateboarding or reading manga?

So when Mrs. O picks me up for church on Sunday, I'm in a bad mood. I didn't bother even to brush my hair; I can feel a giant knot on the back of my head. Grandma Michi notices it before I'm out the door.

"Angela, you can't go out like that." From the bathroom she brings a fine-tooth comb, one of those with a pointy end that could easily poke out your eyeball. She tears the teeth of the comb through my knot. I feel like she's pulling my hair out of my scalp, and tears come to my eyes. Church early Sunday morning is so not worth the trouble.

After my hair knot is untangled and I'm deemed presentable, I get into Mrs. O's car. Mrs. O drives pretty fast for an old person, and within a few minutes, she parks in a lot that's large enough for a grocery store. The church building itself looks like a fancy gymnasium. I don't see any crosses outside anywhere.

Most of the people walking into the church look Japanese, Chinese, or Korean—some kind of Asian. There are a few *hakujin* and even a couple of black people. I'm not used to being around so many Asians so many times a week. In Mill Valley, there are only a handful of us. Of course, when we go south across the bridge to San Francisco, it's a different story. But San Francisco's our weekend world, not our everyday world. I don't know how I would survive in an around-the-clock Asian American world. My own family is one thing. I don't think of them as being Japanese or Asian American. They are just Mom and Dad. Even with my grandparents and the 1001 cranes, they don't seem that Japanese-y to me. I don't feel that we are separate or clumped up like weeds on a nice lawn. But somehow, this church makes me feel a little like an outsider, even though on the outside I look like an insider. I don't want to go in, but Mrs. O is there, her hand on my shoulder.

There're a lot of kids, some really young ones who barely know how to walk. Mrs. O takes us through the building to some open double doors. A chubby man wearing a name tag smiles and hands me a yellow program.

This main room is big, with rows of purple upholstered chairs. I thought all churches had wooden pews, like the Buddhist temple a few blocks away. I want to stay in the back, but of course, Mrs. O steers me to the third row. "I'm a little hard of hearing," she says.

There's a band onstage—a real band, with drums, an electric guitar, and an electronic keyboard. And congas in the corner. I'm getting a little mixed up. Here are Japanese people playing congas in a Christian church.

The music starts and it kind of sounds like regular music that you might hear inside a department store. People standing in the front row, and others sprinkled here and there in the crowd, lift up their hands while they sing. It scares me a little. I've never seen Japanese people acting this way.

Mrs. O, thank goodness, doesn't close her eyes or move her body. But I notice that as she clutches her program, her hands are shaking. The singing finally ends and we get to sit down for a while as we hear announcements. Then the speaker dismisses the children.

"You can go with Keila," Mrs. O says. She has her hand on the shoulder of a slim Asian girl with big brown eyes the size of pennies. They look Asian, but the rest of her face looks kind of *hakujin,* so I know that she's half something else. "She'll take you to your Sunday school class."

"Hi," the girl says. Her voice is soft and comforting, like a favorite pillow.

"You mean I'm not staying with you?" I say to Mrs. O. I sound kind of desperate. I am desperate. I've never gone to a Christian church service and don't know what they will do to me in Sunday school. Dunk me in water? Force me to lift my hands and sing? I don't sing out loud even when I'm by myself. I'm not going to do that in front of people I don't know.

"I can go with you and check you in—"

"It's okay. I'll go with her," I say. I don't want to do it, but at least I'm not going to be a baby and have an old lady as my chaperone.

We walk back out the double doors and I follow Keila down a hall decorated with kids' drawings.

"So are you Mrs. Oyama's granddaughter?" she asks me.

"No. She's just the neighbor," I say.

"Oh. Mrs. Oyama's so nice. I really like her."

Is this girl for real? I think. She has no zits, as far as

I can tell, and even without makeup is beautiful. Her hair is like my mother's, shiny and straight. Even her name is pretty. I'll bet she has lots of brothers and sisters. And parents who are still together.

"I don't really know her." I try to distance myself from Mrs. O. "I'm just staying in Gardena for the summer. Then I'll be back in San Francisco."

"San Francisco—how neat. It's so pretty up there. Do you live near the Golden Gate Bridge?"

That is a nerdy question, for sure, but one I can appreciate. I love the Golden Gate Bridge. I never tire of looking out the window at the persimmon orange cables and beams that hold the bridge together.

"Go over it at least four times a week," I say.

"Wow, you're so lucky." Keila is one of those genuinely nice girls—not like me, with only a thin layer of sweetness on the outside. I wish that I also could be soaked through and through with good and pure thoughts. But I know it's too late for me.

Keila takes me to a classroom at the end of the hall. I sign in and sit on a cold plastic chair with the rest of the girls. There are about nine of them and most are the cliquey, beautiful kind. One, wearing heavy eyeliner and a short cropped top, looks like the main troublemaker. Gazing into one of those free mirrors you get with a twenty-dollar makeup purchase, she adjusts her lip gloss. Five boys are running around, punching a deflated beach ball toward the ceiling. Tony wouldn't be as immature as these guys, I think.

At this moment, I'm glad to be sitting alongside the shininess of Keila. No one can feel completely alone with her.

The teacher—I find out later that he's called the youth pastor—walks into the room. He's young but has a full beard. I can tell by how the other girls look at him, even the troublemaker, that they all have a crush on him. "That's Pastor Barry," Keila whispers, her eyes getting a bit dreamy. Ha, I think, this girl is human after all! Her crush is more grade school than junior high, though. She needs to like somebody who can be a real boyfriend, like Tony.

Pastor Barry makes me introduce myself and no one looks halfway interested except for one of the hyper guys who were throwing the limp ball against the ceiling a few moments ago. "So you're moving here?"

"No," I say in a loud voice that startles even me. "I'm just here for the summer, if even that."

The boy looks disappointed, and I'm surprised. Why would anyone want me to be here, in Asianville? Can't he tell immediately that I don't fit in? But I take his response as a compliment. Maybe I'm not as much an outsider as I think I am.

Pastor Barry then asks the same boy, Nathan, to say some sort of prayer. Nathan looks a little embarrassed and then bows his head. The rest of them, even the troublemaker, close their eyes. I keep mine wide open— just in case. It's like watching a magic show: some don't want to know about the tricks, but I do.

"Dear Lord, thank you for this day. Thank you for everyone who's here, and be with the people who can't be here. In Jesus's name, amen."

Nathan opens his eyes, quickly glances at me, and then turns away.

Pastor Barry then starts telling us a story about Jesus and a woman at a well. She's apparently living with some guy and has a string of ex-boyfriends and ex-husbands. Jesus starts asking her for some water from the well. According to Pastor Barry, Jewish men of a certain class didn't talk to strange women during that time.

"Angela . . ."

As soon as I hear Pastor Barry call out my name, I know that I'm in trouble.

"What do you think about how Jesus approaches the woman at the well?"

Why are you picking on me? I think. I'm new. I shrug. "I dunno," I say.

"You must have some thoughts."

This Pastor Barry is pretty tricky, I think. If I say nothing, it means that I have no thoughts. That my head is empty. Well, I'm not going to fall for that. "It's kind of weird that Jesus asks the lady for water," I say. "Seems like he can get it himself."

The girls in the back start to giggle. If it wasn't for Keila, nodding seriously at my side, I would have done something very unchristian.

"Exactly. Exactly," Pastor Barry says, and he's not

kidding. "But asking for help isn't a sign of weakness. In fact, that's how you build relationships."

The room gets quiet, and I'm not following the pastor. How can asking for help be good in any way? Mom and Dad are always saying that you can't count on anyone but yourself. Gramps says that in camp, he had to *gambaru* on his own. My family's not into help, and come to think of it, neither am I.

As Pastor Barry goes on with his lesson, I picture Mom as that woman at the well. If Jesus came to her asking for water, she would just tell him to get it himself.

At the end of the lesson, Pastor Barry wants to pray again, but this time silently. "God knows all your problems, your struggles. Just talk with him about it."

Everyone bows down again. Again, I keep my head up and my eyes open. Nathan's lips move slightly and I wonder what he's thinking, saying. What problems could he or any of them (besides the troublemaker girl) have?

I finally come up with my own prayer, or maybe it's more of a dare. "If you're really out there, God, then get my parents back together." I don't believe that it will happen, but something deep inside me wants it so badly. If this God knows everything and is all-powerful, then he will be able to do this. That is, if he really exists.

After Sunday school, Mrs. O is waiting for me outside the door.

"Bye, Angela. Maybe we can get together some-time," Keila says to me.

"Yeah," I say, not really thinking it will happen.

"You had a good time?" Mrs. O asks me after Keila leaves to join her parents.

"It wasn't bad."

Mrs. O takes me to a women's bathroom on the far end of the building and tells me to wait outside. There's one closer to the Sunday school classes, but I figure that Mrs. O wants her privacy.

I wait there awhile and then that boy Nathan sees me. I look away, but he heads straight for me. "The youth group is going to go out for pizza and bowling at the beginning of next month," he says. "Maybe you want to come." Nathan is a typical-looking Asian boy. Thin, pale face with a few pimples at his temples. His hair is pine-needle straight and shoots out at a weird angle from his hairline.

"I don't know. I have a job, so I might be kind of busy," I say.

"Well, if you're not doing anything—"

"Yeah, well, I'll think about it."

Nathan walks away and I notice that he's tall. Real tall. At least five feet five inches. He looks slightly un-coordinated, like his legs and arms grew too fast recently. I doubt that he could do any kind of skateboarding.

I wait about ten minutes more, and the crowd

is thinning out fast. I wonder what's going on with Mrs. O.

I finally go into the bathroom. It's tiny, with only one stall. I don't even have to look under the door, because I see Mrs. O lying on the linoleum floor. I get down on my knees. The floor is sticky and I try not to think about why it's so sticky.

"Mrs. Oyama," I say.

Her eyes are open and she tries to get up. "Help me," she says.

I slide underneath the stall door—more stickiness—and edge beside her. There's a little barf floating in the toilet water and a little around her lips. I wipe it away with a piece of toilet paper. The whole time, I breathe through my mouth.

Mrs. O tries to push herself up again, and I wrap my arms around her and lift her. She steadies herself against the bathroom stall and takes some deep breaths.

"Are you okay?" I ask. I know it's a stupid question. She's not okay. Not even close. "Maybe we better call your husband."

"I'm all right. Maybe we should rest a little before we leave. There's a coffeehouse here," she says.

The coffeehouse turns out to be the church's kitchen and a large rectangular folding table. Mrs. O orders a strawberry smoothie for me and a plain water for herself. We sit outside on a couple of folding chairs.

Most everyone seems to have left by now. It's only the two of us on this side of the building.

"You're probably wondering what's going on." Mrs. O presses her dry lips against the edge of a flimsy plastic cup. "I had breast cancer about five years ago. And it's come back."

I suck on my straw and look down. For some reason, my eyes start to blink so fast that I can't see straight.

"I've had to go in for treatments recently. That's why you see me getting ill."

"You still have your hair," I say. My third-grade teacher went through chemotherapy and lost her hair. Instead of wigs, she wore cool long scarves. She is still teaching at my elementary school, as far as I know. She taught us that when you survive cancer, it's called remission.

"Chemo affects people in different ways. My hair just gets curlier, like I had a perm."

"Oh," I say. I don't know if that's good or bad.

"Nobody knows, Angela. Well, except for Mr. Oyama. But nobody else does. Not my sons. Not my daughters-in-law."

I just stare at her.

"I want to wait until after our anniversary party. I want people to be happy and celebrate, not afraid that I'm going to die. Maybe you're too young to understand."

In a way I do understand. Why have a bunch of people worried about you when you have enough to worry about yourself? I don't know about Pastor Barry's theory about asking for help. Mrs. Oyama is a Christian but she's super-private as well.

I don't say much more to Mrs. O. But I do promise that I won't tell. Mrs. O is lucky: I'm the best secret keeper of any girl I know.

# 20

# Loopy Loop

When we get back to 160th Street, there're a note and a phone message waiting for us at Mrs. O's house.

"Your grandparents had to tend to a wedding. I guess it's just you and me for lunch." She smiles. "I hope tuna fish is okay." She goes into the kitchen and leaves me in the living room.

I quickly speed-dial Tony's number. He answers on the third ring.

"Hey, it's Angela."

"Where are you? I've been waiting all morning."

"I had to go to church with the neighbor." I expect Tony to laugh, but he doesn't. "Just do me a favor: call me up right away, okay?"

Tony doesn't ask me why. I hang up and increase the volume on my phone. A couple of minutes later, it rings.

"Oh, hi, Grandma," I say loudly. "Yes, yes. I'll be right there."

Mrs. O pokes her head out from the kitchen. "Is everything all right?"

"My grandmother wants me to go over to the house to finish a project for her." I lie so easily I almost scare myself.

"But you haven't eaten lunch—"

"It's okay. I can just make a peanut butter and jelly sandwich."

Mrs. O looks hesitant.

"I have my own key. She would have talked to you but she's in the middle of a wedding and all."

"Oh yes."

"I'll just wait for Grandma at home."

Even though I told Mrs. O that I could make my own lunch, she makes me wait for her to put a tuna fish sandwich in a small plastic bag. "I'm glad that we were able to do this, Angela," she says, handing me the sandwich.

I nod.

Mrs. O stands on her porch and watches me open our front door. I wave to her and she waves back before going into her house. I feel a little bad, but not that bad, obviously, because I quickly slip into the bedroom to get my skateboard. I leave through the back door and cross our other neighbor's front yard to reach the street.

By the time I'm at the schoolyard, the rest of Tony's friends have left. Tony skates back and forth between the lunch tables, his wheels making long loops of rolling sounds. I skate over to him, and he holds out his hand and I grab for it. It's warm and moist, as though he's been hanging on to a small animal. He speeds up, and I do, too. Even though he's a little taller than me, I can keep up.

We skate like this to the other side of the playground. About three-quarters of the way there, we get out of sync and we have to slow down, but Tony keeps holding my hand. We eventually make it to the end by the handball courts. Tony kicks up his skateboard. "Cigarette break," he says. He takes a crumpled package of cigarettes from his back pocket. He slides a bent cigarette out and, while holding it in his mouth, lights it with a yellow plastic lighter.

I expect him to offer me one, but he doesn't.

"It's a bad habit," Tony says. "It'll make your mouth taste nasty, like an ashtray or even worse. I'm going to quit sometime soon."

We lean against the handball court, its paint and wood peeling and curled up like eyelashes. I watch him finish his cigarette.

"So what are you doing this week?" he asks.

"Just folding, I guess."

"Maybe we can do something. Like go to the mall. Or a movie."

I let the words sink in. A guy is asking me out on a date. For the very first time. I feel that someone has opened a new door in my life. I'm dancing inside. Then

Grandma Michi's face enters my head. I see her pointing at Kawaguchi's and Mrs. O's cranes.

"I don't think I can," I say. "My grandparents have me doing all this stuff."

"Well, I have your phone number. We can stay in touch during the week, at least."

He then holds on to my right hand. Tight. My hand gets sweaty, but it doesn't seem to bother him. His clothes do smell a bit smoky. But not exactly how he described smokers' breath. The smell reminds me of the end of a campfire: warm yet kind of sad at the same time. He then leans into my face. I wonder, Is this it? Is this my first real kiss from a boy? But instead, his lips brush against my cheek. It's quick. He smiles. "I'll call you."

# 21

# Dear Diary

No one's in the house when I get home, and I feel relieved. I go into my bedroom, dig out Mom's diary, and turn to the one written page: *I went to the store today and saw him.*

Again I wonder who "him" is. He isn't my dad; that's for sure. This was long before my dad. I wonder whether he was Japanese or Asian. Or maybe *hakujin.* Or maybe black, or Latino, like Tony.

Did she kiss him? I can't imagine my mother with anyone besides my dad. But then, there was Danny Abraham's divorced father. Danny was in my class last year. He had long hair that he parted on one side; his right eye was practically covered, so I wondered if he could see clearly. One time, when we went to the beach for an end-of-the-school-year party, he fell asleep on his towel and the left side of his face was burnt red, while the right side was still soap white. Mom was one of the drivers on the field trip, and so was Mr. Abraham. He made sure that he sat right next to Mom on the beach, and offered to put sunscreen on her back. (If he's so into sunscreen, why didn't he give Danny some? I wondered.) Mom told him that she wasn't worried about getting burned. It wasn't in her genetics.

All afternoon, he kept looking at my mom. But she ignored him. She is good at ignoring people, and for once, I was happy about it.

Guys don't stare at me like that. Even Emilie gets long looks. Guys instead tell me about their latest skateboard moves or pull my hair and run away. They treat me like their little sister. Until now.

I try to call Emilie, but her voice mail comes on. I think about leaving a message or text-messaging, but announcing my kind-of boyfriend that way is too weird for me. Emilie has kissed a guy before—her boyfriend of three weeks—and now they hate each other. She's kind of bitter, so maybe it's better to keep this news to myself. I imagine myself kissing Tony—this time for real, lips to lips. I roll up my fingers and make a fake mouth with my thumb and my knuckle. I press my lips into my rolled-up hand. I can smell Tony, his sad smokiness. I miss him, I miss him. I reopen Mom's old diary and write underneath her one-sentence entry: *And I can't wait to see him again.*

MICHI'S 1001-CRANES FOLDING TIP NO. 5: The tail should not be folded straight up. It needs to lean at a forty-five-degree angle.

# 22

# Sorry Dojo

After dinner I am lying on my bed, playing a game on my cell phone, when Grandma Michi opens the door without knocking.

"Are you ready?" she says.

Ready for what? I think.

"Ready to go see Rachel?"

I forgot that I had told Grandma Michi I would go with her to the dojo to apologize to Rachel Joseph in person. I don't want to go. I picture a bunch of kids running and jumping and breaking boards. I don't need to witness all that energy before going to bed.

But I don't *monku*. I don't dare. Besides, I've been thinking about Tony. About what it will feel like to kiss him. I think about him holding my face close to his. About feeling the coldness on the tip of his nose. My insides shiver and I feel happy. I haven't felt happy in a long time.

So I don't put up a fight when Grandma tells me to go with her to one of the dojos Rachel's dad works at. He comes to the Gardena one only on the weekend; he helps at another one in a city called Carson.

We drive for about ten minutes and we're right next to the freeway. Giant wooden planters hold baby palm trees. Grandma Michi tells me that the dojo is beside a nursery. It's funny that so much of my grandparents' life is surrounded by plants.

A father and his son, dressed in a *gi*, arrive before we do, and we follow them into a big stuffy room. They both bow when they enter, and I wonder if we need to do the same. So much of being Japanese doesn't involve words or written rules. You have to be quiet and just watch.

Grandma Michi bows deeply in her jeans and San Francisco T-shirt. She looks ridiculous, but no one laughs, so I do the same, only not so deep.

The floor is mostly covered in blue pads, like the ones they use in gymnastics. A slim rectangle on one side holds a wooden bench, where some old men and parents sit. A black woman in shorts sits in the middle. I figure that's Rachel's mother. She probably hates me, I think.

A plastic ice chest is by the door. The walls are all white and free of adornments except for a black-and-white photograph of an ancient Japanese man with a skinny beard and fierce eyes.

"That's our main sensei," an old man tells me before slurping down an A&W root beer. I look into his face; is he the man on the wall? "Have something to drink." He nods toward the ice chest, but I shake my head.

"Hi," says someone sitting on the mat in the corner. It's the girl from church, Keila. Only now her long hair is tied back in a ponytail. And she's wearing a *gi,* with an orange belt around her waist.

"Oh, hi. I didn't know that you do judo." It was a stupid thing to say—I mean, why would that come up in a conversation on Sunday morning?—but Keila doesn't seem to mind.

"I've been studying a couple years. It's a lot of fun."

On the far side of the mat, I see a familiar skinny figure stretching his long limbs. His black hair sticks out from the top of his head like weeds.

"What's he doing here?" I ask.

"Who, Nathan? He's been taking judo as long as me. We went to the same elementary school, too. Now same church, same junior high. We both play for F.O.R."

"What's F.O.R.?"

"It's a Japanese basketball league."

Japanese kids playing basketball? I think they have the wrong sport. Judo makes way more sense.

"Keila . . ." A short, squat Japanese American man calls her. He is wearing a black belt, so I know that he's one of the top guys. His shaved head is white on the top and the sides, like a forgotten tangerine that has gone beyond the rotting stage. His legs are short; his center of gravity is low. He reminds me of one of those round toys you can never knock down.

"That's Rachel Joseph's father," Grandma whispers in my ear as Keila runs to join one of the lines formed on the opposite side of the dojo.

"He's Japanese," I say.

The barefoot kids and men in their white robes take turns twirling like tops toward us on the bench.

"Rachel's adopted. Just recently, in fact. Her new name's Rachel Joseph Akita. That's her adoptive mom right there." Grandma Michi nods toward the black woman.

The line of martial artists now do a strange sequence of somersaults that look like broken wheelbarrows rolling forward.

*Adoptive.* The word sounds funny to me. So un-Grandma-like. It sounds like something a lawyer would say, not someone who makes floral arrangements and folds origami cranes.

It's kind of weird that Rachel has a Japanese father, like I do.

The martial artists now break up into pairs. I'm surprised to see Keila facing a guy at least a foot taller than her. They bow to each other and then start grappling, pulling the front collar of each other's *gi*. I am worried that Keila's *gi* will fly open, revealing her bra and whatever else, but I am relieved to see that she's wearing a purple T-shirt underneath. All the girls, in fact, seem to be wearing something underneath their *gi*.

Rachel is with an older man who must be at least triple her weight. How can she fight him? He could just step on her and squash her like a bug. But somehow she uses what little weight she has and certain twists of her body to pull the man forward. He falls, tucks his head under, and rolls. When he rolls, he slaps the mat hard with the inside of his arm. It sounds like a huge belly flop in a sea of blue padding.

I can't help noticing Nathan grappling with Rachel's father. The men don't wear anything under their *gi*, and Nathan's top opens up, held together only by his green belt. I'm surprised to see that he has some rows of muscle on his skinny stomach. I mean, he's still skinny—I can see his ribs—but maybe he's not as uncoordinated as I thought he was back at the church.

"We are more into *randori* at this dojo," says the root beer man. He has a wispy beard.

"What's *randori*?"

"*Randori* is free style. You just go at it. We don't go over each *kata*, form, again and again. You gotta just experience it, you know." The root beer man is missing some of his teeth, and I wonder who he is.

After fifteen minutes, they trade partners, just like in square dancing. It doesn't matter how old you are, if you're a girl, if you're small; you just randomly get matched up with an opponent. It's obvious that Rachel is one of the stars. Her bows are crisp, and her face determined as she flips and knocks down men, teenagers, and other girls with her foot and arm movements. I know that many of them are just going with the flow; if they were fighting in a dark alley, these big guys would be able to beat Rachel, no doubt. But that doesn't matter here. She knows about imbalance and balance, and I know that I couldn't do what she is doing even if I'd started judo when I started walking.

I look back at Grandma Michi, who's been quiet the whole time. She's watching Rachel with as much pride as if Rachel was her granddaughter. Her eyes are even shining.

The whole session lasts about an hour, and the younger kids stop first. Rachel comes to the side to get a bottle of water from the cooler and finally notices me.

"Why are you here?" She doesn't waste any time getting to the point.

"Sorry," I say. My voice cracks a little. "For getting mad and saying things I shouldn't have said the other day."

Rachel Joseph looks away from me quickly and I'm glad she does. My eyes get wet for some reason.

Grandma Michi nods with approval. I guess I've passed her test.

"You did real good out there," Grandma says, and cups Rachel's head with her hand. Rachel looks like a baby bird with her head and bread-loaf-looking braids nestled in my grandmother's arm.

I can't help feeling a tinge of jealousy. What does Rachel have that I don't? Is it that she's adopted? That Grandma feels sorry for her? Well, what about me? My parents are alive, but they're splitting up. My own family's dying, but Grandma doesn't seem to notice or care.

"Hi, Mrs. Inui. It's so good to see you." Rachel's mother gets up from her seat. She's tall and looks smart, like she could be a lawyer, like my mother, only one who works at it full-time.

"My granddaughter, Angela." Grandma, who's still holding on to Rachel, nods toward me.

"I've heard a lot about you," Rachel's mother says.

I know that might be a bad thing, so I murmur a hello and keep my head down.

Keila comes to the side to get a towel from her athletic bag.

"You should do judo with us," she says to me.

"It's not for me." I don't like to do anything that requires me to wear a uniform. That was why I quit the Girl Scouts. Plus the fact that you have to sell stuff. I don't like asking people to do things that they might not want to do. Mom says I shouldn't take it personally when people reject me. But I do.

"I'm busy, besides," I tell Keila. "I have these one-thousand-and-one-cranes projects." I like saying that now. I feel important. I have a job.

We hear yelling on the mat, and it's Nathan doing *randori* with another boy, who looks like he could be in high school or college. The tops of both boys' *gi* are practically off their bodies as they struggle with each other.

"That Nathan is really going at it," says the man with the missing teeth.

Keila nods. "He never *kiais* so much."

"Ki-yah?"

"*Ki-ai,*" Keila repeats slowly. "It's summoning energy from your insides."

It sounds like just yelling to me.

"I think that he kind of likes you," Keila observes, wiping her forehead with her towel.

I blush, surprising myself. I feel kind of bad, because it should be only Tony who I think about.

"Keila . . . ," Rachel's father calls out again. I have a feeling that Keila gets in trouble for talking too much. I guess she isn't as perfect as I think she is.

"I hope to see you next Sunday," Keila says. She gets up and joins the rest of the robed students, who have now formed four lines.

"*Kiritsu,*" Nathan calls out. The students stand straight as boards and lift their arms forward, like in a Nazi salute, but not quite. "*Rei.*" All of them bow simultaneously.

The session is officially over.

# 23

# First Fight

Tonight Tony calls me. I love hearing his voice. It's husky yet syrupy when he ends his sentences. When he speaks to me, I feel like he's telling me secrets, even though it's everyday talk about helping in his uncle Carlos's store. He tells me about unloading pallets. "Do you know what a pallet is?" he asks me.

"Isn't that something to do with color?"

"I thought you wanted to be a writer." I know what he's getting at. Just like Mom and Grandma, he thinks I'm stupid. I regret telling him that I like to write, although I haven't written anything since my parents started having problems.

"It's not like I know every word in the universe," I say.

Tony senses that my feelings are hurt. "No, no, I'm just teasing. Really. Most people who aren't truck drivers don't know what a pallet is. It's that wooden platform you put boxes of stuff on."

"Oh," I say. I make up my mind not to stay mad at Tony. Did we just have our first fight? I don't know what to do with a boyfriend.

"When can we get together again?" he asks.

"I don't know," I say. Grandma Michi has told me that we are going to have to start gluing Kawaguchi's cranes soon.

While I'm talking to Tony, my mother calls. "I have to take this," I tell him.

"Call me back later."

I press the button to talk to my mother. "Hi, Mom."

"Well, you sound like you're in a good mood."

"Not particularly," I lie.

"Well, I'm going to be out of town for a few days, so stay in touch on my cell, okay?"

"Where are you going?"

"Just taking care of some business."

"What kind of business?"

"Have you spoken to your father?" My mother is good at changing the subject.

"No," I say. Actually, with church, Tony, 1001 cranes, and the judo dojo, I haven't had much time to think about Mom and Dad. And it's felt kind of good.

"He needs to talk to you about something."

My heart starts to race. "About what?"

"He's the one who needs to tell you."

"You brought it up. You can tell me first."

"I'm sorry, Angie. I shouldn't have said anything."

I feel anger rise to my throat. I hate it when my mother does that. "Just tell me."

"No, I can't. It has to come from your father." I don't like how Mom says "your father," like he's not her husband.

"Are you getting divorced? Is Dad going away? Just tell me, Mom."

"Angie, stop whining. I can't stand it when you whine."

"Well, I don't like it when you don't tell me anything!" I'm almost screaming, and I'm glad that Gramps and Grandma Michi can't hear very well.

"Angela. Stop it. I mean it. We will talk about this later."

The line goes dead, and I'm mad. I feel like tearing my room apart, but it's all full of weird equipment. Other than my pillow, there's nothing squishy or soft that I can crush easily. If I hit something, I'll probably end up breaking my hand.

So what's going to happen now? I wonder. I don't bother to change into my pajamas. I stay sitting on the bed in the dark. Tony tries to call me, but I turn my phone off. I want my mind to turn off, too. But it won't.

I sneak out of my bedroom, pass the demon and white-faced masks, and open the front door. The air is still warm; there's a faint breeze and I hear a tinkle of wind chimes from Mr. and Mrs. O's house.

I walk onto the porch and jump down onto the grass. "Here, Nori," I call out. "Tofu, Miso." I kneel and reach for the pie tin. The cat food is all dried up. Aunt Janet, being so busy, must have forgotten to feed the cats.

# 24

# Kawaisoo Cranes

The next morning I sit with Aunt Janet in the 1001-cranes room. I can't believe it, but I've folded all the cranes for Kawaguchi's display. All 1,000. The extra one will be in red origami paper. We'll do it at the very end, says Aunt Janet.

Now we are starting work on arranging the cranes on a black velvet cloth. I feel both excited and a little scared. What if I make a mistake? Before, I could just toss my D and F cranes away. But this is for real. No going back.

Aunt Janet has drawn the design in white pencil. She explains that we have to use math to figure out how many layers of cranes to put in each area. One problem: I hate math. I don't see how knowing what a polygon is is going to help me later in life. Or all that x, y, and z stuff.

"You use math everywhere. Like when you leave a tip

at a restaurant. Percentages—at least learn percentages," Aunt Janet says.

*Yeah, then I can be like you and still live at home when I'm forty years old.* I'm being mean and I know it. I'm starting to sound—well, think—like my mom, and I've been away from her for almost three weeks. I thought I would become less like her as we remained separated, but that's not the case.

Aunt Janet tells me to divide the design, the star, into four sections and then calculate how many cranes should go into each section. I can handle that part—two hundred and fifty. Then she tells me to arrange the cranes, without using glue, in one-fourth of the design.

It sounds easy, but it's not. At first I don't use enough and I have at least fifty left over. I have to start over and pack the cranes more tightly in more layers. Aunt Janet reminds me to use the C cranes in the back. The different grades of cranes are all separated in plastic bags and labeled. At least Aunt Janet doesn't yell at me, like my mother sometimes does. She does suck in her cheeks like Gramps at times, but he doesn't have any real teeth, so he has an excuse. Aunt Janet, on the other hand, doesn't have one.

I finally figure out how many cranes need to be in each row and the distance between each layer. Aunt Janet tells me to write it all down. I do. Next comes the gluing. The scary part. We use white glue that comes in a big bottle with a narrow tip.

"Why does Grandma Michi like Rachel Joseph so much?" I ask while I start gluing the back row.

"What do you mean?"

"I mean"—I take a breath; sometimes Aunt Janet can be clueless—"why is Grandma so nice to her?" And not to me, I add in my mind.

"I guess she feels sorry for her," Aunt Janet says. "Have you ever heard of *kawaisoo*?" She stretches the last part of the word; her lips are a little puckered and her chin is wrinkled like a peach pit.

"*Kawaisoo.* Nope."

"*Kawaisoo* means to feel sorry for someone. Like a homeless lady who smells bad."

So Grandma thinks Rachel smells bad? I think.

"Mom just feels for people who have no families, I guess. Because family is so important to Mom."

"But Rachel has a family."

"Now. But not always. I think she was living with a lot of different foster families."

Now I start to feel bad. And here I told Rachel to go back to her own family. No wonder Grandma Michi got so mad at me.

Later I watch television alone with Gramps (another cop show, but this time we are eating Cheetos). I mention Aunt Janet's *kawaisoo* theory.

"Your grandma seems all tough on the outside, but it's only to protect herself," Gramps says. His dentures are starting to make a clicking sound, so I know it's getting close to his bedtime.

"Protect herself from what?"

"From you. Me. Your mother. People who could hurt her."

"Nobody could hurt Grandma." Not with her wood-like marionette mouth.

"If you only knew," Gramps says, closing his eyes.

Gramps goes to bed, and I finally do, too. I check my phone and nobody has called. I don't even care that Mom and Dad haven't called, but I wonder about Tony. It's nothing, I tell myself. It's nothing. And then I go to sleep.

# 25

# Runaway Randori

The next day Grandma Michi and Janet are off to an anniversary party at a retirement home and Gramps is at the flower shop. I'm by myself in the 1001-cranes room, gluing rows of origami birds onto Kawaguchi's star. I don't mind being alone, because at least I can bring in Gramps's old radio and listen to my music.

About noon, somebody rings the doorbell. I at first don't hear it because of the radio, but the person is insistent. The doorbell is super-loud: Gramps installed a special one that both he and Grandma Michi can hear from every part of the house. My grandmother has given me strict instructions not to open the door to anyone, but I can't help at least looking through their dusty peephole. It's Rachel Joseph's mother, her forehead appearing swollen, like a balloon, through the magnifying glass.

I keep the chain on the door but I do open it a crack.

"Hello, Angela," she says. "Is Rachel here?"

I shake my head.

"Is your grandmother here?"

"She's at an anniversary party. I can call her—"

"No, no, I don't want to bother her."

I see that Rachel's mother is pretty agitated. Her forehead is all puckered and marked with worry lines. She doesn't strike me as a woman who overreacts.

"Wait a minute," I say to her, and close the door so that I can undo the chain and open the door properly.

"Rachel's been missing for a couple of hours. It's been very hard for her lately. Do you know where she could be?"

"She might be at the shop."

"I already checked. No one was there. Just a sign that someone would be back soon."

Gramps must have had an emergency to tend to. Whenever he has to temporarily close the shop, he tapes up the same sign: BE BACK SOON. I tell him that he can order a plastic sign with a clock with hands that can be adjusted to the exact time he'll be returning, but he says that would be too much trouble, messing with tiny plastic clock hands. Besides, he says, he doesn't want to promise that he'll be returning at a specific time.

"She might be in the shed in the back. I think my grandmother said Rachel likes it there."

Rachel's mother looks hopeful.

"You want me to come with you?" I ask.

Before I know it, I'm leaving a message on Aunt

Janet's cell phone (Grandma and Gramps never listen to their messages) and sitting in Rachel's mother's Honda Accord.

"I don't know how much your grandmother has told you about Rachel," says Rachel's mother. She's a good driver who comes to a full stop way before crosswalks and intersections. "We were foster parents at first for several months. We obviously fell in love with Rachel. I mean, who wouldn't?"

I say nothing. I don't know if I need to be older to really appreciate Rachel. My friends have cute brothers and sisters (and some bratty ones, as well), but I haven't fallen in love with any of them.

"The adoption was finalized recently. Your grandmother came to our adoption party."

Well, that figures.

"And now I think that the shock of it has really hit Rachel. She realizes that she's no longer legally her biological mother's child. She's ours."

I don't know why Rachel's mother is telling me all this. I don't know if it's something in my face, or some weird aura I have, but strangers are always revealing their secrets to me. Mrs. O and now Rachel's mother.

On the other hand, I know of only one person down here who I can tell secrets to: Tony. There's Gramps, too, but I can't talk to him about boy stuff. I don't know what he'd do if he found out about Tony. I choose not to think about that.

Rachel's mother parks the car in the back lot and we

both walk to the shed. It's made of old wood that was once painted white, only most of the paint has peeled or worn off. It looks like it belongs in a movie about pioneering families moving west, not in the middle of Los Angeles. The combination lock, the round kind that you can find on lockers, is open. I pull the door's green handle, and sure enough, Rachel is sitting on the ground between some plastic buckets and a shovel.

"Rachel, I was so worried about you." Rachel's mother pushes me from behind and kneels down to hug her.

"I was waiting for Auntie Michi."

"Auntie Michi's not here, honey. You know you can tell me anything."

"Auntie Michi understands. She understands me more than anyone else."

# 26

# Astronauts and Alstroemeria

Before we climb into the Honda, Gramps shows up in his white van. I guess Aunt Janet was able to contact him, because he knows what's going on.

"We found her in the shed," says Rachel's mother.

Gramps grunts. "You have to be careful," he says to Rachel. He then notices her tearstained face. "A lot of sharp tools in there," he says in a softer voice to Rachel's mother.

"Thank you so much, Angela," Rachel's mother says to me, and then turns back to Gramps. "Should I take Angela home?"

"No. In fact, I may need her here."

Rachel's mother waves goodbye while Rachel just stares at me from the passenger seat. What did she mean that only Grandma Michi understands her? I saw Rachel's mother cringe a little when Rachel said that, and I cringed a little inside, as well.

"There was a big mix-up," Gramps then tells me. "I don't know what Janet was thinking. She wrote that the Carrillo party was next week, when it's actually today. I had to call in some favors to get these flowers." Gramps unloads from the back of the van some carnations, daisies, roses, and other flowers I've seen but don't know the names of. A few bunches are wilted around the edges, and Gramps tells me to peel off those petals.

"You're going to have to help me make some arrangements."

I've never done that before, I think. But then, there are a lot of things I'd never done before coming to Gardena.

Gramps takes me to the battered sink in the back room. Here he's stacked green foam bricks.

"This is called an oasis." Gramps makes me pick one up, and they are as light as Styrofoam. "It's called an oasis because it holds in water. I'll cut them; you soak them." He places a stopper in the sink and turns on the water full blast. He begins chopping each oasis brick in half, and I punch holes in them with a chopstick before dunking each one into the water until the air bubbles stop coming out. We work quickly, like an assembly line. Gramps then stuffs a wet oasis into a plastic-lined container. "I'm going to show you how to make an arrangement. Watch closely, An-jay, because you'll be on your own for a while."

"Where will you be?" My voice takes on a high-pitched tone.

"I have to pick up some more flowers from my friend in Montebello. I'll be back in an hour and a half."

I'm feeling a little desperate again, but I think, *Gambaru, gambaru.* This is no big deal. I can do it. "Okay, Gramps," I say.

"Good girl," he says, smiling. He takes out an old kitchen knife and slices the wet brick in half again. He puts the cubed oasis into a gold plastic bowl, taping it down with floral tape. I don't see how this thing is going to look nice, but I keep quiet.

There are rows of flowers and greens in front of him on the table, which is covered with newspaper.

"These are alstroemeria." He points to flowers that kind of remind me of baby tiger faces. The outside petals are orange, but a couple of the yellow inside ones look striped.

"Astro-what?" The name of the flower sounds like "astronaut" or a word for something else that spins in space.

"It's also called a Peruvian lily."

They have superlong stems, and Gramps explains that when the flower growers pick them, they pull them out of the ground rather than cut them. The flowers last longer that way.

I like the first, fancy name and ask Gramps to repeat it. Alstroe-meria. Alstroe-meria. I chant it in my head as Gramps clips the greens and sticks them into the oasis. Next come the carnations, the roses, the daisies, and the alstroemeria. After Gramps is done, the arrangement looks beautiful.

"Do you think that you can do this?" he asks.

I nod, not really sure I can. But I am going to try. I promise to keep the doors locked and not to let anyone in.

Gramps picks up his keys from the table and smiles. "An-jay, you're a good girl," he says, and leaves.

Doing the arrangements is a lot easier than folding the cranes. The first one doesn't turn out very well, but if you mess up, you can pull out a few flowers and stick them back into the oasis in a different spot.

I'm on my fifth arrangement when my phone rings.

"What are you doing?" It's Tony. "Working on your origami?"

"No, I'm helping to make some flower arrangements at my grandparents' store."

"Hey, I'm only a couple blocks away. Can I help?"

"I don't think so. I'm here by myself. My grandpa won't like it if I let strangers in."

"I'm not a stranger." Tony sounds a little hurt.

"You know what I mean. A stranger to him."

My excuse doesn't work on Tony, and about ten minutes later, someone is rapping on our front door.

I unlock it. "Listen, you can't be here. I'll get in trouble."

Tony ignores me and walks into the shop. "This place is pretty old. As old as my uncle's store."

"Doesn't need to be all fancy. We sell flowers, live things, not shoes or T-shirts." I don't know why I'm being so defensive. I wasn't that impressed with the store when I first walked in. I go into the back room and he follows me.

"No, no, I'm not saying it's bad," says Tony. He comes closer to me. He then pulls up my hands and puts them on his shoulders. "I like it. And I like you."

He leans in and my heart leaps. His lips touch mine and I feel like I'm falling into a deep hole. The kiss ends before I know it, and I'm looking straight into his face. We're so close that he looks like he's become a Cyclops.

I lean back, and he smiles and holds my hand. I'm glad that I brushed my teeth two times this morning. His lips didn't taste that ashy and I wonder if he's already started to quit smoking.

I don't know how long we stand there, holding hands. I've left the world of green foam oases and entered a place that's wilder and more alive. I don't hear the jangle of the front lock, the bell on the top of the door, the footsteps.

"What is going on here?" a voice snaps, finally bringing me back to Gardena. Grandma Michi, standing next to Gramps at the door.

Tony and I immediately let go of each other's hands and back away from each other as if a magnetic field has repelled us.

The worst is Gramps's face. His eyes look empty, and his mouth is slightly open, like his dentures got stuck in an uncomfortable place. I lower my head.

Grandma Michi drops her packages onto the curdled-coffee-colored linoleum. They are obviously heavy, because they make a clunk when they hit the floor. "Thank God your mother is coming down this weekend," is all she says.

MICHI'S 1001-CRANES FOLDING TIP NO. 6: When you make the head, first fold it down on one side. Then open it back up and press down in the center, and you should have a perfect head.

# 27

# Grounded

I've never been grounded before. Emilie's been grounded a couple of times. I've read about it in books and seen angry parents in movies yelling "You're grounded!" But that's not my parents. I get punished by their being disappointed in me. I usually get the full-name treatment from Mom: "Angela Michiko Kato . . . I want you to think about what you've done." "This is not like you," is what Dad says. They don't scream or yell. It's like they are each throwing a rock down a long, dry well: the rocks then just bounce back and forth against the sides, making lonely sounds.

When they started not getting along, I thought maybe my bad grades or back talk would somehow fuse them back together, but instead I felt their lonely disappointment two times over.

But now Grandma Michi says it: "You're grounded. You can't go anywhere by yourself, and when you leave the house, it can only be work-related. And no seeing, no talking, no anything with that boy again."

Gramps says nothing. He can't even look me straight in the face. Disappointment. Gramps's disappointment is ten times worse than being grounded.

Like my grandmother said, my mother will be back in town. It really has nothing to do with me and Tony, because she was planning to come down anyway. But now I have to be prepared to feel her disappointment in me, too.

The next day, when Gramps drives me to the shop, the expression on his face is the same. His eyes don't turn up in a smile like they normally do. I wish that I could tell him how Tony has helped me. How he saved me from Kawaguchi's wrath. How he made me feel special when my parents seemed to be abandoning me.

But it's too late for any of that. I've lost something with Gramps, my only lifeline in Gardena besides Tony. I just remember his smile when he left me in charge with the Carrillo flower arrangements. "An-jay, you're a good girl," he said.

Gramps leaves me in the back room of the shop, where I'm supposed to be gluing cranes for Kawaguchi's wedding. They don't trust me in the house alone anymore.

I look at the stack of dry oasis bricks and feel like crying. Only yesterday Gramps felt that I was responsible enough to make real floral arrangements on my own.

I hear the bell on the door ring and then hard, definitive footsteps against the linoleum. A female voice and then Gramps's reply. More hard footsteps, and then a figure is standing in the doorway. Kawaguchi, in a pantsuit this time, but with the same pearls. "I was in the neighborhood, so I wanted to check on the display."

I move my hands away from the black velvet so Kawaguchi can get a good look. My fingers are sticky from the glue, and I rub my thumbs against my second and third fingers.

"This row doesn't look even," Kawaguchi says after a few minutes of studying the display.

It's fine, I'm thinking, but I tell her that I can make some adjustments, because the glue is still wet.

I hear the bell on the door jingle again, and figure it's another customer. But it turns out to be someone completely different: the Buddhist minister, who Gramps directs to the back room.

"What are you doing here?" Kawaguchi asks.

"You said that you'd be stopping by here before the rehearsal. I need to talk to you alone."

I try to shrink into the corner. The minister doesn't even care that I'm in the room. Kawaguchi's eyes follow me for a second but focus back on the minister. She doesn't seem to care, either.

"Are you sure about this? I mean absolutely sure. I'm not talking about us and what happened. But you and Kevin. Are you sure about him?"

"Of course I'm sure about him. We're getting married in two days. All the arrangements have been made."

"Forget about the arrangements. The hall. The reception. The flowers and this one-thousand-and-one-cranes display. I'm talking about your life, Lisa. Is this where you want to be?"

"This is so not right. What are you trying to do to me?"

"You tell me that this is it, Kevin's the guy for you, and I won't say anything more. I'll support you through everything. I'll make it the best ceremony I've ever officiated."

Kawaguchi's chin trembles a little. I notice it but I'm not sure the minister does. Then Kawaguchi's face becomes as still as stone.

"Yes, I'm sure about this. A hundred percent sure." Her voice is steely.

"Okay," says the minister. "Then I'll see you at the rehearsal." He walks out, and a few seconds later, we hear the bell ring.

Kawaguchi's chin is trembling again, and her eyes seem shiny, but not a good shiny.

"Okay," she echoes, but to me. "The cranes look fine."

# 28

# Small Talk

I am looking forward to doing nothing when I get home, but when Gramps pulls into the driveway, we both notice one of those new versions of old-fashioned cars parked along the curb. It's the color of gourmet mustard, kind of light, not like the regular mustard you put on hot dogs.

Gramps and Grandma have hardly any visitors come over, I've noticed. Maybe it's because they're so busy at the shop and at the weddings of strangers.

When we go through the back door, it's no stranger sitting at the worktable of the 1001-cranes room. It's Dad—only his hair is cut all choppy and he has some gel in it. Dad never puts stuff in his hair. He doesn't even use conditioner.

I'm happy to see him, but something stops me from running up and hugging him. "Hi, Dad," I say instead. I feel shy around him, like I'm meeting someone I used to be close to but I'm not anymore.

"Angie." Dad gets up and presses my head into his shirt, a new one that's deep blue. "I've missed you."

I've missed him, too, but I think I've missed what we used to be more. He has his cell phone hanging from his belt, and I wonder why he hasn't called me if his phone is right there.

Dad then greets Gramps. "Nick," he says, extending his hand.

Gramps doesn't take a hold of it, spreading out his palms. "Dirty from flowers," he says, but that doesn't seem like a good excuse. That never kept Gramps from shaking another person's hand. He takes off his work boots and leaves them on a towel where our other shoes are stacked.

"Janet let me in. She went to buy some groceries."

Gramps just grunts and then says he has to get cleaned up. He leaves me alone with Dad.

"So I've heard that you've been busy," he says. I know he means Tony.

"Is that why you came?"

"I'm just here for the day on business. But I knew that we had to talk."

We sit at the 1001-cranes table. The stacks of photo albums have been moved to one side. In their place are three piles of golden cranes. The B pile is the biggest, but the A pile is slowly catching up.

"You did all these?"

I nod.

"You have been busy."

I know that Dad is just making small talk. "He's not my boyfriend or anything like that," I then announce, although in my heart I hope Tony is. "Just a new friend I met skateboarding."

"I know we've never talked about dating and boys. But twelve is way too young to be alone with a boy, Angie."

One part of me wants to argue, but another part is relieved. The relieved part wins out, I guess, because I nod, knowing that I'll still find a way to see Tony.

Dad clears his throat. "There's actually something else I wanted to talk about with you. . . ."

I wait. My heart is pounding. I know what he's going to say. *We're getting a divorce.*

"I know it'll be hard for you to understand, but I want you to know that this isn't about you. It's not your fault."

Just say it, I think. I want to blurt it out myself so this talk won't be so long, but I'm not going to give my dad an easy out.

"You might hear that I've made a new friend myself."

Friend? That's my word for Tony, although he is anything but just a friend.

"She's actually the mother of one of your classmates. Joanne Papadakis."

I feel like my stomach has been punched in. Mrs. Papadakis? She was my room mother when I was in third grade. She has hair the color of sand and a long nose with lima bean nostrils. I can see Nicole Papadakis, her curly long hair and invisible plastic braces. "Is Mrs. Papadakis your new girlfriend?" My voice is so soft I can barely hear it myself.

Dad doesn't say anything. I think back, and it slowly starts to come to me: how Mrs. Papadakis seemed always to be sitting next to Dad at school plays. How he seemed always to have a last-minute meeting on Fridays, when he was supposed to be off. How Nicole Papadakis never seemed to like to talk to me.

"How long has Mom known?"

"Let's not talk about your mother and me," he says. "What I really care about is you and me."

But I start thinking about Mom. Why didn't she give me at least a clue to what was going on? Why didn't she warn me? I feel like this is all coming out of nowhere, and I'm not prepared.

"I don't know what's going to happen, Angie. I just need some time to think. But since Nicole's one of your classmates . . ."

I wince. I don't want to think about it, but the images creep in: the girls at school talking about me and my dad behind my back. Dad and Mrs. Papadakis, in a white dress, underneath a white gazebo, getting married. Nicole, smiling up at my father with her braces, saying "Dad."

The 1001-cranes room begins to spin. All the shimmering gold and silver seems harsh to me. I can feel the points of the tips of the origami cranes. I need to get out of here.

"Is there anything else?" I ask.

"What?" My father looks confused.

"Do you need to tell me anything else?"

"Just that I love you, Angie. And I always will."

I get up from the folding chair and escape to the bedroom.

I lie on the bed for a while and then check outside. The new old mustard-colored car is still there. I can't help creeping through the living room to see what Dad's doing now.

I hear Gramps's voice from the 1001-cranes room. "I don't know what's happening, and I don't know if I even want to. But An-jay has to be your number one priority," he says. He sounds serious, possibly even angry. Maybe Gramps can be the one to get my parents back together.

Dad then says that he needs to make his flight. The bottom of his folding chair scrapes the linoleum floor.

I run back into my bedroom and watch through the window as he drives away.

# 29

# Pessimist Club

Friday evening I go next door for dinner. I try to get out of it, because I'm in no mood to talk to anyone, especially the O family. Even though they are much nicer and more polished—at least on the outside—than our family, it's just more of the same. Nobody in either family says anything real. Gramps doesn't even mention anything much about my dad's visit.

Grandma Michi tells me that I still have to go to dinner. "You made a commitment; now you have to follow through," she says. How come other people can break theirs, but I have to keep mine? I think. But it's not worth arguing. I'm so tired I just go along.

She tells Aunt Janet to walk me to the O family's door, just in case I try to take a detour to see Tony. Aunt Janet actually just waits in the middle of the walkway, looking at me like a stray dog.

Mr. O answers the door. He's in a suit and he explains that he has to go to an Optimist Club meeting. I know what an optimist is: it's someone who always sees the good side of things. I can definitely picture Mr. O as a member of an Optimist Club. It must be nice to be in the company of all those optimists. I'm the opposite; I'm a pessimist. But I wouldn't mind being surrounded by optimists from time to time.

"I better get going, Ruth," he says to Mrs. O, straightening his jacket collar. "Don't want to be late." If he is late to a meeting, he explains, he is fined seventy-five cents. Seventy-five cents is nothing, but it's the principle of the thing, he says.

The other men are also not at dinner. The two brothers have gone to a bachelor party for their cousin.

"So that leaves us girls," Mrs. O says. Her voice sounds too high and too loud, as if she's adjusting her volume to convince herself that we're going to have fun. I don't think we're going to have fun, but then, that's the pessimistic side of me coming out.

The dinner is quiet. We're eating lasagna, home-made, not the frozen kind from a box or one from the warehouse store.

Sarah clicks her teeth with the ends of her fork as she eats. Apparently, it bothers Helen, because when Mrs. O excuses herself from the table, Helen snarls at her, "Can you stop that?"

"What?"

"That noise. The fork hitting your teeth."

"I'm not making a noise."

"You are. Isn't she, Angela?"

They both look at me and I shrug. I don't like getting in the middle of girl fights. That Sarah and Helen are practically old enough to be my mother doesn't make any difference. Girl fights don't seem to change much over time.

It finally dawns on Sarah that Mrs. O has been away from the table for a long time.

"What's happened to Mom?" she asks no one in particular. She gets up and we watch her walk through the living room, to the hallway where the bathroom is.

I hear her knock on a door. "Mom, are you okay?" she asks.

Helen rises from the table, too, and I follow. I think I know what's going on, and I'm worried about Mrs. O.

We all stand in front of the locked bathroom door, and I can hear Mrs. O throwing up. It doesn't sound like the little barfs she's done before.

Sarah taps again. "Mom, can you unlock the door? Let us help you."

"Is it the flu?" Helen asks.

I don't know whether to say anything. The toilet flushes and then we hear water running from the faucet.

"Maybe we should take her to the hospital," Helen says to Sarah.

The doorknob turns, and there's Mrs. O, drying her wet face with a hand towel. Her eye makeup is smeared and she looks awful.

"No, no, I don't have the flu. And I don't need to go

to the hospital again." She walks down the hallway to the bedroom where I saw Mr. O massaging her back.

"Mom, what's going on?" Sarah calls out.

Mrs. O turns. "My cancer's come back, damn it. And I'm going to rest," she says, and then closes the door behind her.

Now, if anyone else had said "damn it," it would have been no big deal. But this is Mrs. O. Even though I haven't known her that long, I know she's not the type to curse, or even sort of curse.

"Did you know about this?" Sarah asks Helen.

"Did you?"

"Nobody knew," I say. "Except for Mr. O." I don't say that I knew, too, although they can figure that out.

"This doesn't make any sense." Sarah wanders back into the living room and slumps down on the couch. Helen walks out from the hallway and then turns to me. "Why do you know?"

Sarah waits for my response.

I'm not sure. "It just sorta came out. She's gotten sick in front of me before."

"You should have told somebody," Sarah says.

"Don't blame her; she's just a kid." Helen comes to my defense.

I don't like how this argument is going. First of all, Sarah is accusing me of having done something wrong when Mrs. O explicitly told me to keep a secret. And Helen is saying that I'm just a kid, which is also wrong.

Before I can stop myself, I'm speaking. "She wanted

you to be happy, at least until the anniversary party. She didn't want anyone to worry. And I think she wanted you guys to try to be friends, at least for a short time." My voice isn't squeaky like it normally is when I speak to grown-ups. It's low and steady. It sounds like me.

Sarah and Helen stare at each other.

Helen then plops herself down at the dining room table. "Hit me with them, then," she says.

"Huh?" I ask.

"The origami papers. If three of us work together all night, maybe we can finish."

So as Mrs. O rests, we fold. By the time Mr. Optimist returns from his meeting, we are close to having six hundred cranes, separated into three distinct piles on the table.

Mr. O seems to sense that something has changed, and I know I should leave as soon as I can.

When I'm home and I get into bed, I text-message Tony and he answers me. Grandma Michi and Gramps don't know about these things. They kind of understand how you can send messages and read messages on the computer, but they don't know that you can talk on the phone without really talking.

Tony asks me if it's okay to call, and I tell him no. But I text-message him that I'll call him. And I do, when everyone's gone to sleep. Just in case, I cover myself with a sheet and a blanket, and I stuff the pillow close to my face.

I whisper into the phone that I can't talk long. I think about telling him about my dad and Mrs. Papadakis but then decide against it. Saying it aloud will make it more real. And I want to pretend that it's not true, at least for a little bit longer.

"When can I see you next?" he asks.

"Well, I'm kind of grounded." It's actually not "kind of." It's for sure. But I want to see Tony. "I'll be at a wedding tomorrow. At the Buddhist church."

"Are your grandparents going to be there?"

"No, I'll be with my aunt. Besides the 1001-cranes display, we're also doing the boutonnieres and the bridal bouquet."

"Maybe I'll pretend that I'm in the wedding party."

I almost start laughing. There's probably no one in Kawaguchi's life who looks like Tony.

**MICHI'S 1001-CRANES FOLDING TIP NO. 7:**
If you make a mistake, you don't have to throw the crane away. Save it, because you may be able to use it in the back layers.

# 30

# A Change in Plans

I've never been to a wedding before. My dad's an only child, like me, and Aunt Janet has never been married (and has never had a boyfriend, for all I know). So we don't have a lot of relatives who have gotten married since I've been alive.

Aunt Janet has told me that we don't have to dress up for the wedding, because we're the workers, but that I still shouldn't wear jeans or shorts. She tries to get me to wear one of her denim skirts, but it's so loose around my waist and my butt, it looks more like a sleeping bag than a piece of clothing. I go into my mother's closet, and I find a simple pink and yellow plaid shift in the back. It's sleeveless and definitely old, but in a cool, retro way. And it fits perfectly. Even Grandma Michi is impressed. "You look like a young lady," she says before picking up her purse to meet Gramps at another event. I bring along my blue Hawaiian-flower-pattern mini backpack. I know that it clashes with my dress, but I don't care.

I help carry the 1001-cranes display to the trunk of the car. It's all framed and wrapped in black felt. It's my first one, and even Aunt Janet says that I've done a good job. We have to stop by the shop on our way to the wedding, to pick up Kawaguchi's bridal bouquet and the men's boutonnieres. She told Gramps that she was going to make her bridesmaids' bouquets, which Gramps secretly thought was a bad idea. "Customer's always right," he muttered to me after he'd tried to talk her out of it.

The boutonnieres are simple. They each have one white flower against a green leaf. The flower is called stephanotis. They have petals that are long and delicate, and they look like wax trumpets. Kawaguchi's bouquet is full of stephanotis and white roses. It looks so perfect that it doesn't seem real.

On the ride to the Buddhist temple, Aunt Janet tells me a lot of things I know and don't know about weddings. Like that it's bad luck for the groom to see the bride in her dress before the ceremony. Even though I've never gone to a wedding before, I know that much. I know that brides should wear something borrowed, something blue. But then she tells me that if it rains on someone's wedding day, it's good luck for the marriage. That doesn't make sense to me. I look out the car window, and the sun is already bright. Doesn't look that lucky for Kawaguchi.

The parking lot is already full, so I wonder if we are late. After Aunt Janet parks, she thrusts the box with the bridal bouquet into my arms. "You find the bride and I'll pin the men," she says.

"How about the one thousand and one cranes?" I ask. I want to make sure that everyone sees it.

"That's later, for the reception," Aunt Janet explains.

As we rush up the stairs, I see a familiar figure in a plaid button-down shirt and khakis. Tony waves, and my eyes dart back and forth between him and Aunt Janet, who's just concentrating on finding the grooms-men. I point to the front of the steps, meaning that I'll be back as soon as I can. Tony nods.

We find the wedding coordinator, who directs me into one room and Janet into another. The room I enter looks kind of like a library, only there's a huge mirror in front of some old books in Japanese. Kawaguchi is sit-ting in a padded chair, her head down. I'm surprised, because she really looks beautiful. Her dress is strapless and shows off how thin she is. Her hair is piled on top of her head, and her makeup isn't overdone.

Before I can say anything, I notice that someone else is in the room. The groom. Kevin. I've seen him only one time, and that was in a car with Kawaguchi. He looks like a younger version of Mrs. O's sons, clean-cut and tall. There's a whiteboard on wheels right in front of the door, so they don't seem to notice me. I think about tiptoeing back outside, but I don't want to move.

"What are you saying?" he asks.

"I can't marry you."

My mouth falls open. I can't believe what I'm hearing. Neither can Kevin. "What?"

"I can't do it."

"Lisa, our whole families, our friends, coworkers—they are all out there. And you want to call this off?"

"Reverend Marc—he was my boyfriend in college. We were even talking about getting married."

"Why didn't you tell me? We could have gone to a different church. Gotten a different minister."

Kawaguchi just sits in her chair. Frozen. I begin to feel sorry for her.

"Are you saying that you still have feelings for this guy?"

"It's not that. I just can't figure out why I couldn't tell you the truth. From the beginning."

I can't believe what's happening. How do people know when they've found the one—the one who lasts forever? Did my own mom have any doubts when she got married holding fresh wildflowers? What made Dad like Mrs. Papadakis? What makes one better than the other?

Someone knocks on the door, and both Kawaguchi and her fiancé look back, finally noticing me standing there with the box of roses and stephanotis in my hands. The door opens, and it's the minister. He's wearing a long robe the color of mustard. "Everyone ready?" he asks.

# 31

# Big *Haji*

Aunt Janet says that the Kawaguchi wedding was the biggest disaster she's ever witnessed. She's on the phone with Grandma Michi, and I can hear only Aunt Janet's side of the conversation.

"She goes in front of the sanctuary, in front of everyone, all the guests, the parents, and says that they've called the wedding off. *Haji.* Yeah, big *haji.*"

My ears perk up and I wonder what *haji* means. Nothing good, most likely.

"Yes, canceled. So what are we going to do about the flowers? I know, I know. They still owe us half of it. Yeah, I'll make sure. And the one-thousand-and-one-cranes display. Same thing, huh?"

I forgot about the display; does this mean that it's all going to waste?

"I have to make sure. I mean, it's not our fault that they didn't know what they were doing." Aunt Janet sounds huffy, almost betrayed. I've never heard her angry before.

"Aunt Janet, what's *haji* mean?" I ask after she ends her conversation with my grandparents.

"A shameful thing. A very shameful thing." She then turns and walks toward the sanctuary with a strong sense of purpose. I'm alone, and I'm grateful. I find Tony where I left him, in front of the temple. He's making figure eights on his skateboard. He stops when he sees me, and I notice that he has rolled his long-sleeved cuffs up to his elbows.

"So what happened?" he asks.

"The bride called off the wedding."

"No way."

"Yeah." I still can't believe it myself. To see Kawaguchi, once all perfect in her white dress, standing in front of their guests, her face red and swollen . . . The fiancé had already left. He told her it was all her doing and she would have to clean up after herself.

Kawaguchi hasn't been very nice to me, but at that moment, I saw a different side to her. It was as if someone had peeled off that hard plastic layer and revealed a soft bloody heart, like in those medical television shows. Her sad face made me think of my mom. Maybe that's how Mom feels inside, too.

"You look nice," Tony says, stroking the edge of my neckline.

I pull on the straps of my backpack and am aware that I have to be careful. Who knows who might be driving down the street? We move to the edge of the temple by some mint green trees. We hold hands for a little while, and then Tony lets me go.

"I have to get back to my uncle's store. He's getting a shipment in, and I promised that I'd help unload."

"A pallet, huh?"

"Yeah, a pallet." He smiles. I'm happy we have some inside jokes—lame ones, but still.

He squeezes my hand and then he leaves. I wave to him from the top of the temple stairs and watch him skate down the street, his long hair flying back.

I then hear a voice. "Angela Michiko Kato. Is that who I think that was?"

# 32

# *Urusai* Mama

I knew that Mom was coming down to Los Angeles. But I didn't realize that she would get out of her jeans and change into a sundress and heels to go to Kawaguchi's wedding and check up on me. Needless to say, I'm in trouble—big trouble.

My grandparents in the Bay Area, Jii-chan and Baa-chan, have another word besides *"monku"* that they use all the time. It's *"urusai."* Like when Baa-chan bothers Jii-chan for the tenth time about fixing a leaky bathroom faucet. *"Urusai,"* he'll snarl back. And if he's in a really bad mood, he'll mutter, *"Urusai* mama." *"Urusai,"* which sounds like "OO-ru-sai," means "annoying," "nagging," or, generally, "Get off my case."

So standing there at the top of the stairs of the Buddhist temple, I take a big breath and get ready for a huge blast of my own *urusai* mama.

First she aims her anger at Aunt Janet. She tells

Aunt Janet that I'm a kid (yeah, the kid thing again) and that I need supervision. She pratically blames her for my sneaking around with Tony behind everyone's back.

Then—this is what surprises me—Aunt Janet fights back. "I'm not her mother. I'm her auntie. She's not my responsibility. You should be the one who watches her."

I'm shocked that Aunt Janet has spoken up like that. And so is my mother.

Mom whips her head back to me. "I'm really, really disappointed in you. And where's your cell phone? I'm here now; you don't need your cell phone."

I open my mini backpack, pull out the phone, and lay it into her open palm. I don't know how Tony's going to reach me now, but at least I know his number and the number for his uncle's store.

While the three of us are arguing, a groomsman wearing a wilted stephanotis boutonniere comes up to us and timidly asks about the 1001-cranes display. I guess the fighting of three Japanese females from the same family could scare off a pro wrestler. "They told me that I'm supposed to take it," he explains.

Aunt Janet takes a breath and frowns at Mom. "You come and help, Angela," she says, and my mother nods, giving me permission to move. We go to my aunt's car and she pops open the trunk. When we hand the display over to the groomsman, I feel sad. My beautiful display probably won't be seen by many people—if any. And for Kawaguchi, it'll be a reminder of all that went wrong rather than right.

# 33

# Cinnamon Yellow

I am a prisoner the next week.

Mom doesn't want me even to go to the shop, so I stay in the back room, gluing cranes onto Mr. and Mrs. O's anniversary display. Their design is much more difficult; there're bamboo and cherry blossoms, and I'm not sure if it's looking very good.

I'm sleeping on the couch again, because Mom took back her own room. She says she's going to stay in Los Angeles for a little bit because she has some business to take care of. It makes me suspicious, because what kind of business would Mom have? It's not like she has a serious full-time job. Back in Mill Valley, she goes into the city only three times a week, and she's always home by the time school ends.

Mom keeps trying to talk to me—like really talk—but I'm not used to it. So whenever she tries to sit me down, I run away. She finally gets me early in the morning, before breakfast. I'm not a morning person and she uses that to her advantage.

"Dad talked to you, I heard."

I nod and fold my arms around the top of the sleeping bag. The zipper scratches the inside of my right arm, but I don't bother to move.

Mom's eyes fill up with tears, and it scares me. I don't think I've ever seen her cry. If Mom falls apart, what will happen to me? "Do you have any questions?" she asks.

I shake my head. I do want to tell her that I need to see Tony. He's the only one I can really talk to. But she wouldn't understand.

Mom says that I can share her room with her and sleep on the floor on a blow-up mattress, but I tell her I'm better off sleeping in the living room.

"You talk in your sleep," I lie. "You did last time here."

"I do not," she says, but then she stops herself, because we both know that she doesn't have anybody in her life to tell me I'm wrong.

I start writing Tony little notes on small yellow Post-its. They are actually one- and two-word poems: "Miss You," "Cinnamon" (the way he smells—smoky and sweaty and sweet, all at the same time), "Smile," and "Yellow" (the way the world looks after I see him). I keep all the Post-its in my mom's old diary, which I've hid between the couch cushions. My mother is watching me like a hawk and even going through my backpack, so I figure this is my private secret code. Once I'm let loose, I will make those words into real poems or, better yet, tell him in person.

I'm writing one of my secret notes when the doorbell rings. I wait for my mother to answer, and after a few minutes, she calls my name.

Mrs. O is standing on the other side of the open doorway. She's looking much better than she did the other night, and I'm relieved. "The youth group at our church is having a bowling party," she says. "I know that it would be so nice if Angela could go. One of our girls—Keila Harmon—has been asking about her."

"Is this a coed activity?" My mother has her arms crossed and I'm surprised that Mrs. O hasn't softened her one bit. Mrs. O is a little like Keila; she seems to bring out the best in even the crabbiest people. Or at least people try to put on a nice fake front for her. But not my mom.

"Why, yes. Is that a problem?" Mrs. O wrinkles her face. "The parents are invited, too, you know."

I'm not that interested in bowling, but it would be nice to get out of the house, even if it was with my mother. So when Mom finally agrees to allow it as long as she chaperones, I'm actually looking forward to it.

# 34

# Turkeys

The bowling alley turns out to be a cool retro one, with a neon sign. When we open the heavy glass door, I hear the crash of bowling pins punctuating the whizzing and beeping of video game machines. And I smell cigarette smoke mixed with the scent of french fries from the snack bar.

It's not hard to find the youth group. There are only about twenty lanes in the whole place, and maybe four of them are taken up by Asian teenagers. For some reason, I notice Nathan first. He has just finished rolling his ball, throwing it forward like he was doing a softball slow pitch. It bounces on the wood lane and then gathers speed, punching the pins down like loose teeth. All fall except for one, in the back corner, hanging around like an actor stubbornly refusing to leave the stage. Nathan's immature friends yelp and groan, and he shakes his head and gets ready for his ball to return.

"You came!" Keila's in front of me on the checker-board linoleum floor. She's really happy to see me.

"Angela, what size shoe do you want?" my mother calls, waving me over to the rental place. A man stands behind a glass case with new bowling balls and bags on display.

"I dunno. Six, I guess."

"You're lucky; you have small feet. Not monster ones like me." Keila points to beat-up red bowling shoes that have a large number eight on the back.

"You must be Keila," my mother says. "I'm Angela's mother, Ms. Inui."

"I thought your last name was Kato." Keila's large eyes widen.

"She kept her maiden name."

"Oh," Keila says, and then smiles.

I then wonder if that was my mother's intention all along: to keep that former part of herself in case marriage to my dad didn't work out.

Keila links arms with me and takes me to a booth where triangles of cold pizza lie in open boxes.

"Nathan's here," she says.

"I have a boyfriend," I say.

"You do?" Keila seems surprised. "At your school?"

"He actually lives here. His name is Tony."

"Why didn't you invite him?"

"He couldn't make it," I say. I don't want to get into having been caught kissing and being grounded. For some reason I care about how Keila sees me: as a better version of myself.

Keila helps me look for a bowling ball with a good fit. I always feel funny about sticking my thumbs into the holes of neon-colored bowling balls. Who was using it before me? When you rent the shoes, they spray the ragged insides with Lysol. The alley needs a little spray for the thumbholes, I think.

I finally go with a neon pink ball, eight pounds. Keila's impressed; hers is only seven pounds. But she has skinny matchstick arms. Mine are like stretched-out turkey drumsticks, meaty and solid.

"Angela's on my team," Keila calls out to the others. Pastor Barry is sitting in front of the scoring computer and nods to me.

We can't have two girls on the same team," Nathan says to Keila. I can tell that they've known each other for a while, because he speaks to her like she's his younger sister. Angela's on our team."

"Nathan's right, Keila," Pastor Barry says, and before I know it, he's pressed "AK" on his keyboard and I'm set to bowl after "NC."

"Oh well." Keila's disappointed.

I sit down next to her and pull off my Vans. I'm happy that I brought an extra pair of socks. The insides of my size-six bowling shoes are all worn, and when I slide my feet in, they feel slightly damp and warm.

"It's the Lysol," Keila says, wrinkling her nose.

"Well, whose team am I on?" Mom asks. I forgot about my mother. I thought she was going to sit back with the cold pieces of pizza. But that wouldn't be Mom. She likes to be where the action is. She has already picked out a sleek midnight blue ball that looks like it's brand-new. "Didn't know I did my share of bowling in high school, did you, Angie?" Mom says to me. "I've even bowled here a few times when this alley was practically new."

Pastor Barry stands up. "You're Angie's mom? I'm Barry, the youth pastor."

"Karen." My mother extends her hand, and I'm dismayed. Mom is never this friendly. Has she, like the rest of the girls, fallen for Pastor Barry?

"You can bowl on our team," he says.

"I thought two girls couldn't be on the same team," I say.

"Angie, I'm not one of you girls," Mom slips off her flip-flops and takes a pair of short athletic socks from her purse. She stretches out her legs so that everyone can see her painted toe nails before she covers them with her socks. I'm so embarrassed.

It's four of us—Nathan, me, and his two friends—against Pastor Barry, Keila, two other boys, and Mom. I'm the lousiest bowler on my team, and Nathan's friends rub it in. "She needs a handicap. Give her fifty extra points," they say after I roll my third gutter ball.

"Angie, you're twisting your hand. Stretch out your arm, let go, and aim your thumb towards your nose."

My mother tries to coach me from the chairs on the other side.

Hit your own nose with your thumb, I think.

Keila cheers me on even though she's on the other team, and Nathan just says I have bad luck. He sticks out his balled fist toward me and I wrinkle my nose. "Press your fist against mine," he says. I don't know what that's supposed to prove, but I do it. I guess it means "too bad" or something like that.

Nathan, or "NC," is a really good bowler. He gets a couple of strikes. Everyone cheers—even the other teams—and he high-fives us all. When he touches my palm, I notice that his hands feel callused—maybe from the grappling in judo?—and then I feel ashamed. I'm Tony's girlfriend; why am I thinking about how another boy's hand feels?

Pastor Barry turns out to be an even better bowler. He gets a turkey, which is three strikes in a row. A cartoon turkey even blinks on a video screen above. Everyone cheers again and I notice that he high-fives Mom with both hands instead of just one.

We play two games. They win one and we win one. I end my second game with an 84, which isn't bad, because Keila gets a 70. I almost suspect that Keila started getting gutter balls just so I wouldn't feel bad, but she says that her arms were getting tired. When she shows me her swollen red thumb, I finally believe her, and we go to the bathroom together to wash our hands.

"Yuck, the lanes are so dirty," I say, spreading out my

fingers, which are practically black. We take turns squirting soap into our hands, and the water turns gray with the dirt.

"Too bad Tony couldn't make it," says Keila.

"Huh?" I've almost forgotten that I told her Tony's name. "Yeah."

"You know . . ." Keila gets close to me. "Nathan really, really likes you."

"How do you know?" My cheeks become flushed.

"Because he told me. I didn't know what to say to him—you know, because of Tony. But I just wanted to make sure that you and Tony are together-together."

I step back from Keila. "What, you think I'm lying?"

"No, no, it's not that. I've just never met him. I think Nathan is so much better."

"If you've never met Tony, how would you know?" I grab some paper towels from the dispenser. I'm not liking Keila anymore, and my real self is starting to show. "And anyway, you don't know me. You don't know anything about me." I throw the paper towels toward the trash can, but I miss. Keila bends down to pick them up and I take the opportunity to leave.

Pastor Barry is talking to my mother at the table with the pizza boxes. She's way too old for you, I think. And she's married.

"Mom, I'm not feeling well."

"It must have been the pizza, huh?"

"I'm really feeling bad."

Since I usually don't say things like this, Mom takes

me seriously. "Well, nice meeting you, Barry," she says, and shakes his hand again. "I'll be in touch with you about that other matter."

When we are in the car, I finally ask her, "What other matter?"

"What?"

"What's that other matter you were talking about with Pastor Barry?"

"Oh, you heard that."

I hear everything you say, I think. "So what were you talking about?"

Mom adjusts her jacket and tightens her grip on the keys in her hand. "How would you feel if we moved down here?"

"What do you mean?"

"If we moved to L.A.—I'm not talking about Gardena specifically—on a more permanent basis."

"What do you mean—you, me, and Dad?"

"No, just you and me."

"I would think that it would be awful. Terrible."

"But there are girls like Keila. Nice girls you could be friends with."

"She's not that nice," I say. "And I miss Emilie." I do miss Emilie, but I suddenly realize that we haven't talked once this summer. "I miss our house," I add, and it's true.

"There're plenty of nice houses here in Los Angeles. Besides, I thought you were starting to get used to it down here."

"But it wasn't for forever. I can't live here for forever."
I picture our house in the woods tumbling down, falling apart.

"Just try to keep an open mind, Angela."

I don't know what Mom is talking about. I kept an open mind about being away from my parents and staying with Gramps, Grandma Michi, and Aunt Janet. About the 1001 cranes. About going to church. Meeting new people. What more does she want from me?

"I know it's been hard for you. But it's been hard for me, too."

Now did my mom want me to feel sorry for her? In a way, she must have created this, I think. With all her *monku*, all her stubbornness. She must have driven my father away. This time I don't cry. I don't shed one tear.

**MICHI'S 1001-CRANES FOLDING TIP NO. 8:**
The last crane, the 1001st one, should be red for good luck.

# 35

# *Obon* Dance

Every July I go to the Obon festival in Berkeley, across the San Francisco Bay, near my other grandparents' house. Baa-chan dresses me up in a cotton kimono called a *yukata* (not "yuk-ata," but "you-kata") and wraps a bright red tie-dye sash around my waist. I love the sash. It is soft—softer than a pair of stockings, and a lot tougher, too. Baa-chan even puts makeup—well, only mascara and lipstick—on my face.

Usually a drummer wearing white shorts, a *happi* coat (looks like the top half of a kimono only manly), and a cloth tied around his head bangs on a huge *taiko* drum. The sound is so loud and deep that you can feel it in your chest and even down to your fingertips and toes. Really. Dancers circle the drummer. Some of them wear fancy kimonos, while others just dance in jeans and T-shirts.

I watch the ones in the fancy kimonos, because they

know all the steps to the dance. For some dances, you need a round fan and a long, skinny towel. For others, you need these things called *kachi-kachi,* which are red and blue castanets. If you really know what you are doing, you get to use red-painted curved bamboo things.

The Obon in Berkeley is fun, so when I hear that Grandma is going to a practice for the Obon dance at the Buddhist temple, I tell her that I want to go, too. It's been a couple of weeks since the bowling party, and I've almost finished Mr. and Mrs. O's display. Gramps will soon be starting to frame it in the back room. I know that it will turn out even better than the Kawaguchi display. "Good job," Gramps says, his head partially down. He doesn't look at me straight in the eyes much anymore, and when he does, it's like he's looking through me, not at me.

I keep writing Tony my secret notes, and I've used four Post-it pads in the process. Every time we're in the car and we pass his uncle's store, or the middle school on a Sunday, I search for a sign of Tony. He has no idea that my cell phone has been taken away and my mother is watching my every move. She even disconnects my grandparents' phone at night and puts it on the side of her bed, against the wall, when she goes to sleep.

I have another reason for wanting to go to the dance rehearsal. Like in those old-time cowboy and Indian movies, maybe the drumming will somehow bring Tony to the Buddhist temple. He's always skateboarding around town; wouldn't a bunch of Japanese people dancing in a circle outside draw him and his friends over? Just in case, I bring my three Post-it pads' worth of words, my poems for Tony, in a plastic bag.

Grandma Michi, Mom, and I all go to the practice. Aunt Janet says that she needs to work on an order in the shop. Gramps says he feels a little tired, but I know that he's not into dancing. Usually I'd tease him, but I don't dare to now.

The practice is held on the church's outside concrete basketball court. Some old ladies in blue *happi* coats are already there. It turns out that most of the people are old—really old, like my grandparents' age. Most of them are women, too, except for one man who's dressed in a *yukata*, even though it's just a practice, and another guy in jeans, who stands by a *taiko*.

"We're going to start off with the *tanko bushi*," a woman, the instructor, calls out. There's a CD player on a table next to the *taiko*. The woman, who wears a cotton *happi* coat and false eyelashes, presses down on the Play button.

I recognize the music. It's happy and lively and I like how it makes me feel inside.

"This is called the coal miner's dance," the instructor explains. A circle forms around her and the *taiko* drummer. The ones who know the dance start on the steps right away. Grandma stands beside me so that I can follow along.

"Right foot forward first," she says. "Dig, dig." She

moves her arms together two times as if she's sweeping the floor in front of her. We repeat on the left side.

Then she bends her right elbow back toward her shoulder and does the same on the left. Grandma explains to me that we are throwing coal into our baskets. I didn't even know that Japan had coal.

We then stagger backward a couple of times—apparently the basket is pretty heavy—then push, push, and finally open our arms as if we are spreading coal on the ground. (Seems pretty messy, if you ask me.) And then clap, clap. Clap.

A woman is singing our dance song on the CD and I love it when she calls out *"a yoi yoi."* It sounds and feels like a yo-yo going back and forth.

We do this song until our circle goes around two times. Then we learn the gardeners' dance. The instructor explains to me that some of the songs and dances were created by Japanese Americans, not people in Japan. I can figure that out because the gardeners' dance song is in English. Grandma says that her father and Gramps's father were both gardeners. I can't imagine them having fathers, or maybe I can't picture either of them being a kid, like me.

Next is a dance with the long, skinny towels. The dance has a Japanese name, but I'm not sure what it is. Grandma has brought towels for all three of us, but Mom hasn't been practicing with us. Instead, she stands by the drinking fountain, talking to some lady who looks about her age.

We start off with the towels hanging loose from our necks, like we are champion runners after a race. I'm a little nervous, because I've never done the towel dance before. The music comes on, and we hold the towels out in front of us with two hands, like they're a sacrifice. Only I'm not doing it right for some reason. The movements go fast and I'm getting lost.

"No, no, Angela, not like that. Don't hold the towel so tight." I see the crease between Grandma Michi's eyes.

I try again and she corrects me. "No, Angela, not like that. How many times do I have to go over it with you? You're so slow sometimes."

Her words burn through me. I'm feeling the past weight of all her criticisms related to my origami folding.

I stop in my tracks, even though everyone else is moving. "Why do you always have to be so mean to me?" I say. I don't realize how loudly I'm speaking, but it's enough for the dancers around us to give me funny looks.

"What are you talking about?" The cotton towel is resting on Grandma's left shoulder now.

"Why can't I do anything right? And why do you have to be so fake and such a bad grandma?"

Grandma Michi's marionette mouth drops open. My heart starts racing as if it needs to be somewhere else in a hurry. My feet start moving and soon I'm in a full-out run.

The happy music keeps playing as I go through the metal gate. My mother must have finally noticed, because I hear her call out "Angela!"

There's no question of where I'm going: Tony's uncle's store. It feels good to run free and be away from my family. Away from their problems. My problems.

I'm happy to see the mold green structure, standing out like one of those castles in a goldfish bowl.

Sweat is dripping from the tip of my nose, and I brush it away with the cotton towel. I stop when I reach the doorway and my eyes have to adjust to the darkness of the store's insides.

I expect to see Uncle Carlos behind the counter, but instead, it's Tony, wearing a red T-shirt with the name of a band on it. I'm so happy—I can't believe it.

I start to say something but he's not alone. An Asian girl with long, straight hair is handing him some liter bottles of soda to stack behind him. She doesn't seem to belong inside the liquor store. She's too pretty to be working there and she doesn't look like a relative. She purposefully gives him four bottles, and Tony's overloaded. He drops one, and the plastic container bounces on the cement floor like a bowling pin. The top must have gotten loose, because the bottle bursts open and soda starts to shoot out on the floor. "You—" He tries to grab the girl's waist but she squirms away with a fake laugh. A girlfriend's laugh.

Tony grabs some old newspapers to soak up the

spilled soda. He kneels down and then looks up toward the doorway, noticing me for the first time.

"Angela," he says as if he is apologizing. The girl squints at me.

My head is still pulsating from my run. I am so stupid, I think. I thought things that happened to my friends, like Emilie, wouldn't happen to me. I'm never the reckless one. I'm the one who thinks things through carefully, the quiet one who doesn't act on impulse or emotion.

"I've been trying to call you," he says.

I take a few steps back, onto the sidewalk. "I hate you," I whisper. He probably can't hear me, but I mean it. I hate every part of him.

My feet start moving again and I'm halfway down the block.

I hear Tony. "Angie, I'm sorry."

*Sorry, sorry, sorry.* That word falls into itself and circles like the revolution of skateboard wheels.

# 36

# Hot Tears

The tears are dropping hot and heavy again. I hate my tears. I hate that my face and my eyelids are going to be swollen again, revealing my feelings for all to see. I hate Tony. I hate Gardena. I hate my mom. I hate Grandma. And I really hate my dad.

The cranes. I hate the cranes. I hate having to fold every last one of them. I hate how Grandma Michi forces me to make them perfect. But nothing's perfect, Grandma.

I tear the key from around my neck and try to open the back door. I want to go through that way because they are there: the cranes. The stupid cranes. I want to crush them. Tear up Mr. and Mrs. O's 1001-cranes display. What does it mean? Nothing. They are just a lie, like everything else.

I'm finally able to unlock the door and I can see the

origami birds shining like gold points on black velvet. Before I can get to them, I notice something else. On the other side of the display is Gramps, hunched over in a chair, with sweat streaming down his face. "An-jay," he murmurs, "help."

# 37

# Flat Soda

My hands are shaking and I'm at the phone, calling 911. "My grandfather thinks he's having a heart attack," I say. The operator asks me for our address, and I can barely remember it, but read it off some bills next to the phone. The operator then asks me if Gramps can move both sides of his body. I put the phone down and check and then go back. "Yes," I tell her. "And he can see okay."

I listen to what the operator says next and finally get off the phone. I run into the bathroom and open the medicine cabinet, which, like everything else, is completely filled—pill bottle stacked upon pill bottle. But I finally find what I'm looking for and run back to Gramps. "Take this." I hand him an aspirin. I don't know what it's supposed to do, but I follow what the operator told me to a tee.

I try to call Mom's cell, but just get her voice mail. "Come home," I say. "It's an emergency."

I go back to the other room and kneel next to Gramps. "The ambulance's coming," I say.

I go into the kitchen, fill a plastic container with a built-in straw with water, and bring it to Gramps. He tries to take a sip but the water just ends up spilling over his face.

We hear the front door opening. "Angie . . . ," Mom calls out.

"Mom," I call back.

Mom and Grandma are now in the doorway of the 1001-cranes room.

"What the—" Mom hurries to Gramps's side. Grandma Michi steps back and I'm afraid she's going to faint.

"It's my heart, Grandma," Gramps calls out.

Grandma Michi steps forward and takes a hold of Gramps's hand—I've never seen them touch each other in this way—and he keeps telling her that he's okay and the ambulance is on its way.

"Oh no, oh no," my grandmother murmurs. Her voice isn't shrill or loud. It's as flat as old soda that's been left out too long.

# 38

# Dental Floss, Anyone?

Grandma Michi gets in the ambulance with Gramps while Mom and I go in Mom's car to the hospital. My fingertips are as cold as ice. In the mirror on the passenger-side visor, I notice that my face looks greenish.

Mom, surprisingly, is super-calm, and she even manages to smile a little. "It'll be okay, honey," she says when she stops at an intersection. She doesn't seem to say it for me as much as for herself.

We go into the emergency room and Mom waits in line for a few minutes. "We'll have to go onto another floor; you might have to be in the waiting room for a while," she says.

We take an elevator and Mom tells me to sit in a waiting room that has a television set mounted on the wall. A family is watching a program in a language I don't understand. Two of them are boys, probably around six and seven, and they are carrying half-empty plastic containers of Gatorade, one neon yellow and the other blue. They are bored out of their minds and whine and pull at each other's T-shirts.

There are some magazines in a corner and I leaf through them, but they are all super-old, with the best places to golf in Scotland and tips about how to make traditional Christmas decorations.

After a half hour, I see a familiar face peering into the waiting room. It's Mrs. O, wearing white slacks and sandals that show off her painted toenails. Before I can ask her what she's doing here, she slips into the plastic chair next to me. She squeezes my wrist. "I spoke to your aunt Janet," she says.

Mrs. O doesn't follow that up with anything else. She doesn't say that it's going to be all right, because we both really don't know. She just looks around the waiting room—a box without any windows—at the loud television set, the brothers, and the old tattered magazines. "Not much to do in here."

I nod.

Mrs. O rummages through her purse, which is as fat as an old-time doctor's bag. "Look what I have." She holds up a package of origami paper. "Kept extra ones just in case."

Mrs. O takes the golf magazine and places it on her lap as a makeshift table. I sit cross-legged on the floor.

"This will be for your grandfather," Mrs. O says as she begins to fold. "Our little origami prayers."

I fold on top of the decorating magazine and I'm surprised by how easily I can make cranes now. Mrs. O's a little slower than me, but she makes sure that her folds are razor sharp, just the way Grandma likes them.

The family takes a break from the noisy television set to see what we are doing. The whiny kids with runny noses slowly creep closer and closer to me, and Mrs. O nods to them and hands them each a crisp golden folding paper.

And soon I am teaching them, step by step, what to do. We go through Mrs. O's origami paper, so I open my plastic bag of Post-it poems and use those squares to fold, too. You can't see the full words anymore, just "Y-E" in "yellow" and "M-O-N" in "cinnamon," but I like it better that way. When we are done with those, we begin tearing the pages of the old magazines to make more squares. I feel like I'm doing something wrong, but Mrs. O started it, so I suppose it's okay.

We finish folding more than a hundred cranes; they aren't A-or even B-grade, but good enough. Now what? I think, and Mrs. O can read my mind. She goes into her purse again and finds a needle-and-thread kit, but the leftover thread is only about three inches long. She dumps all the contents of her purse onto an empty chair: wallet, about ten pens (all capped), toothbrush with a plastic cover, checkbook, cell phone, a couple of green tea bags, and finally, dental floss, mint-flavored.

"Aha," she says, picking up the dental floss dispenser. "This will work."

She tells the two boys to open up the cranes, and I'm supposed to poke the middle of each one with the needle. One of the brothers is a little rough and pulls the wings too hard, tearing one of the magazine cranes. He looks like he's going to cry, but I tell him it's okay. "There's plenty more."

Mrs. O then takes each crane and threads them together with the dental floss. You can tell that she's organized, because she doesn't assemble them in just any old way, but creates a pattern, as if she is making a beaded necklace. Three gold ones, one yellow Post-it, two magazine ones. It makes me laugh to see a little man golfing on one of the wings.

Mrs. O makes three strands of cranes: two short ones for the two boys and a long one, which she hands to me after she threads the last crane.

Mom and Aunt Janet finally come to get me in the waiting room. "Gramps wants to see you," my aunt says, and Mom tells Mrs. O that Gramps will have bypass surgery tomorrow.

Mrs. O puts all her junk back into her purse and waves goodbye to me. "I'll see you back home," she says, and leaves. I forget to say thank you, but figure she understands.

As we leave the waiting room, I see my grandmother turning the corner in the hallway and coming toward us. She stops in midstep when she sees me. She starts to say something but then keeps walking. I hear her sturdy sandals slap the linoleum with each step. Mom remains quiet for once. It's Aunt Janet who says softly, "She's still in shock."

I walk into Gramps's room by myself. Mom waits outside and says I shouldn't stay long. I carry in the threaded origami cranes. I don't know where to put them, and first start to wrap them around the plastic guardrail on one side of Gramps's bed, but he shakes his head. "Those doctors and nurses will crush them. Hang them from that board over there so I can see them." He's talking about a small whiteboard on the wall. Someone has written his name, Nick Inui, and a few numbers beside it.

"Beautiful," says Gramps. "Just what I needed."

"Are you going to be all right, Gramps?" I ask. The room smells yucky, vinegary and like medicine. I would never want to eat anything in that room.

"They are going to operate on me tomorrow. It'll take some time, but I'll be like new."

Grandma Michi walks in. "You better get some rest," she tells Gramps.

"Yah, yah, don't worry, don't worry. Just need a little more time with An-jay."

"You shouldn't get worn out." She keeps standing there. I know she means that I should leave, but I stay where I am. "Two more minutes," she states before leaving.

"Do you know that you're my hero?" Gramps says.

I wrinkle my forehead.

"That aspirin might have saved my life."

I just did what the operator told me, I think. But I still feel warm and happy to be called Gramps's hero.

"Grandma and I got into a fight," I tell Gramps. "Back at the Buddhist church. I told her that she was a bad grandma."

"Oh, I see."

"I think she's still mad at me."

Gramps shakes his head. "She's just worried about me. I'm all she has."

"But there's us," I say, meaning me, my mom, and Aunt Janet. And even my dad.

"It's just that she's never had much of a family."

I'm shocked that Gramps is saying this to me. Family is everything to Grandma Michi, Aunt Janet told me. It means crests and big parties, doesn't it?

"Your grandma is afraid of being alone. She has a lot in common with you. She knows exactly how you feel, An-jay. She never had two parents living together."

"What?"

"Her parents weren't even married, ever. She grew up in an orphanage with other Japanese children."

"In Japan?"

"No, here in Los Angeles. It was in a place called Silverlake. It was run by someone from Japan."

I breathe in what Gramps has said. No wonder

Grandma Michi knows so much about Japan; she probably learned it all in the orphanage. And no wonder she and Rachel Joseph have a special connection. "Do Mom and Aunt Janet know about this?"

Gramps shakes his head. "No. Just me and you know." And Rachel Joseph, I think. "This can be our secret," he adds.

"But why? Why does everything have to be a secret?" I'm sick of secrets and I'm sick of being the secret keeper. Grandma Michi is so old, anyway. What does it matter that my grandmother's parents weren't married and she lived in an orphanage?

"You don't understand, An-jay. With some people, what other people think is almost more important than what they think of themselves." Gramps takes a big breath and I wonder if his heart is starting to ache. "I'm not saying that it's good or that it's right. Some folks just like to keep quiet about their personal life."

"It's sure not the *hakujin* way." Or the Christian way. I think back to the story of Jesus and the woman at the well.

"But it's our way, your grandmother's and mine. You need to find your own way, An-jay."

"What am I going to do about Grandma? I don't think she even wants to talk to me."

"She loves you. You're our only grandchild. Do you know how precious you are to us?"

My eyes get misty.

"She wants to know you, talk to you. But she doesn't know how to do it with words."

How can you talk to someone without words? I think.

"I'll talk to her. But you'll need to talk to her, too," he says.

So much for silent ways, I think.

# 39

# Silent Roosters

When Mom and I are driving home, she tries to stop by a sandwich shop near Tony's uncle's store, but I tell her that I'm not hungry. I don't need any reminders about Tony right now.

After Mom parks the car in the empty driveway, we go into the house through the front door. It seems so lonely now. Yeah, the fireplace is still crowded with the *kokeshi* dolls and the roosters, but something seems to be missing. Even the masks by the front door seem wooden and lifeless.

Mom goes into her bedroom and closes the door. I hear her talking on her cell phone. I sit down on the couch and surf some television channels. Nothing seems to take my mind off Gramps and Grandma Michi.

After a while, Mom comes out and stands in front of me. In her right palm is the red cell phone. "I've decided to give this back to you," she says. "I think somebody's been trying to reach you." She then goes into the kitchen, and I hear her opening cupboards and taking pans out. I look at the cell phone display. 5 MISSED CALLS, it reads. They all are from Tony's phone number; two of them were made today. I don't feel like listening to his messages. I might feel differently tomorrow or the next day or the next, but I still erase the messages one by one. I can figure out what he's going to say, and it really doesn't matter, especially now.

I turn the phone off, zip it into my backpack, and watch more TV. After an hour, I reach underneath the couch cushions. I find Mom's diary stuffed between them, and tear out the page my mother wrote about seeing some guy at a store.

I go to the first page after the diary title page and start to write. I begin from the time Mom and I were on our way down from Mill Valley to Gardena on Interstate 5. I write about my first days at my grandparents' house this summer, Mr. and Mrs. O, even the cats that Grandma is not supposed to know about. I write about all the secrets people have told me. And finally, I write about how I feel and what I'm scared of.

What is real love—you know, the kind that's supposed to last forever? I want the kind that I can hold on to tight, that won't disappear. I didn't think Tony would disappear, but he did. And I never thought Dad and Mom would get a divorce, but it looks like they might. How did Kawaguchi know that guy wasn't for her?

I chew on the back of the pen for a while, and then keep going.

> Nothing really seems to be the way it is supposed to be. But some things are actually a little better than they seem. Like how Gramps really, really cares about Grandma more than I ever realized. And how Grandma really, really cares about Gramps. They're not all kissy-kissy, but I guess that's only one part of it.

I write a few paragraphs more and then Mom calls me for dinner. She says that she doesn't care if I'm not that hungry; I still need to eat. Before I go to the bathroom to wash my hands, I leave the diary in front of Grandma Michi's door. I find a yellow Post-it and write on it *To Grandma. From Angela.* I then add *P.S. I'm sorry.*

# 40

# One City

Somebody's knocking at the front door, and the clock next to the *kokeshi* dolls says it's ten. Aunt Janet woke me up earlier this morning, but I obviously went back to sleep on the couch. I'm not sure who else is home, so I finally pull myself up and go to the front door in my bare feet. I open it, and there's Dad.

He's wearing jeans, a crumpled T-shirt, and sunglasses. I wish I had a pair of sunglasses, because the sun is bright.

"How is he?" he asks. I find out that Dad has been driving all morning.

"I think he's in surgery now. I'll get Mom," I say, and turn, but he grabs me by the arm. "I want to talk to you first."

We decide to take a walk and I don't even bother to brush my teeth or comb my hair. I'm even still wearing my pajama bottoms, but Dad doesn't care. He doesn't care about what people look like on the outside.

"I heard that you practically saved Gramps's life," he says.

I'm surprised that the news has reached him. "I just did what the 911 operator told me to do," I say.

"But you followed through. Following through is so important." We walk underneath some smog trees and I can't believe that I ever thought they were ugly. I love everything about Gardena right now—the floating hedges, the smell of salt water. "I guess I've really let you down," Dad says.

I don't try to make him feel better by saying *No, you haven't.* I can't let him get off that easily.

"How long has Mom known about Mrs. Papadakis?"

"A while," he says, and I start feeling bad for my mother. Tony ripped my heart out, and he wasn't even a boyfriend. I can't imagine what it would have felt like if he had been someone really important, like my husband. "But I didn't want to talk about me and your mother. This is about you and me."

Dad says that he's been doing some soul-searching and that he's not going to be spending as much time with Mrs. Papadakis, but he explains that he's not going to be moving back in with us, either. "I think I have to be on my own for a little while. But that doesn't mean I won't be seeing you. We'll get together all the time."

I nod, but I think, That is, if I stay in Mill Valley. I'm still not quite sure where home will be for me. Even if I go back to Mill Valley, it's not going to feel the same. I have barely spoken to Emilie, and besides, I feel that I've changed so much this summer I'm not the same person anymore. I'm not sure who I am or if I like who I am. The parts of my brain and my heart that remember kissing Tony or folding the 1001 cranes will never disappear. And although some of it hurts, I wouldn't give any of it back.

# 41

# The Last Crane

It's funny: when I first came to Gardena, I knew no one besides Grandma Michi, Gramps, and Aunt Janet, but now a small crowd of new friends gathers in the waiting room while Gramps has his surgery. Rachel, Rachel's parents, Keila, Nathan, and, of course, Mr. and Mrs. O.

Something is wrong with the air-conditioning in the waiting room, so everybody's face is a bit red and jackets are off. My dad and mom are there, too, even sitting next to each other in those uncomfortable plastic chairs. They really aren't talking much, but it's good to see them together. I wonder if maybe my prayer at church has come true, but not exactly in the way I pictured it.

Aunt Janet isn't around, because she had to go to the flower market in Gramps's place. But before she left, she squatted down alongside the couch, next to my head on the pillow. "Let me know when Gramps gets out of surgery," she said. She spoke to me like I was an adult, not a kid. Although I wasn't totally awake, I nodded. I'd remember.

Keila comes up to me and links arms with me as if everything is fine between us. Nathan leans against the wall and glances at me from time to time. Mr. O squeezes my shoulder. Rachel Joseph's parents just smile. Rachel shyly comes up to me and presents me with a homemade card.

"I'll give this to Gramps and Grandma Michi," I tell her, but she shakes her head.

"This card is for you."

It's made out of colored cardboard and tape. When I open it, some paper flowers pop out. Underneath the crooked bouquet are the words "I hope you feel better."

I'm not sure if she's talking about Gramps or my parents' separation, but it doesn't really matter. Rachel has written my name on the card in capital letters, and it feels good that someone is thinking of me.

"Thanks," I say, but she's already gone to her parents.

I haven't seen Grandma Michi all morning, and my heart feels very heavy, as if it's overloaded with sandbags and rocks. I don't know if she had time to read my diary or, if she did, whether she liked it. She didn't stay in the waiting room, and I heard that when Gramps's surgery was over, Grandma was the only one allowed to see him.

I notice that Nathan has moved around the waiting

room's walls, like an arm of a stealth clock, and now is only a couple of feet away from me.

"You know, I just may be staying in L.A.," I say to him.

"Oh, yeah?" he says, and a huge goofy grin spreads over his face. Nathan is definitely not cool, but I like that he doesn't hide how he feels.

Grandma Michi walks through the doorway. She's wearing no makeup, and her hair is all frizzy and unkempt. "The operation went well," she announces, and it's like the whole room lets out a group sigh of relief. "The doctor says Nick should be fine."

Everyone's waiting to talk to Grandma Michi, but she heads straight for me. "I read your diary," she says. "It was very well-written." She reaches into her purse and takes out a gold box, which she shoves into my hand. She gestures for me to open it.

Sitting on a pillow of cotton is a red origami crane. It's miniature, no bigger than Mom's wedding ring.

"Oh, the good-luck crane for Mr. and Mrs. O's display," I say. "It's so cute."

But Grandma Michi shakes her head. "This one is for you. And I'm sorry, too." She then grips my hand for a second, and I feel like sparks fly from her touch. Sweat begins to drip from Grandma's nose and the top of her lip. The same way I sweat.

Someone pulls Grandma aside to get more details about Gramps's surgery, leaving me with the gold box. I study my gift and see how it's different from the thousands of cranes we have folded for the wedding displays: instead of being closed, this good-luck crane is fully open, its wings spread out wide, ready for wherever the wind will take it.

# How to Fold a Paper Crane

Begin with a square piece of paper—ideally one side colored and the other plain. Place the colored side faceup on a table. In all diagrams, the shaded part represents the colored side.

**1.** Fold diagonally to form a triangle. Be sure the points line up. Make all creases very sharp. You can even use your thumbnail.

**Unfold** the paper. (Important!)

**2.** Now fold the paper diagonally in the *opposite* direction, forming a new triangle.

**Unfold** the paper and **turn it over** so the white side is up. The dotted lines in the diagram are creases you have already made.

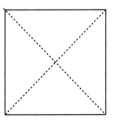

**3.** Fold the paper in half to the "east" to form a rectangle.

**Unfold** the paper.

**4.** Fold the paper in half to the "north" to form a new rectangle.

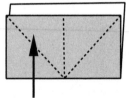

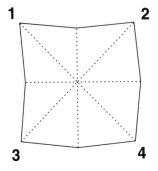

Unfold the rectangle, but don't flatten it out. Your paper will have the creases shown by the dotted lines in the figure to the left.

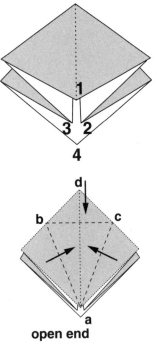

**5.** Bring all four corners of the paper together, one at a time. This will fold the paper into the flat square shown to the right. This square has an open end where all four corners of the paper come together. It also has two flaps on the right and two flaps on the left.

**6.** Lift the **upper right** flap and fold in the direction of the arrow. Crease along the line **a-c**.

**7.** Lift the **upper left** flap and fold in the direction of the arrow. Crease along the line **a-b**.

**open end**

**8.** Lift the paper at point **d** (in the diagram above) and fold down the triangle **b-d-c**. Crease along the line **b-c**.

**Undo** the three folds you just made (Steps 6, 7, and 8). Your paper will have the crease lines shown to the left.

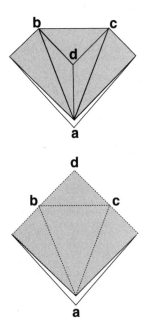

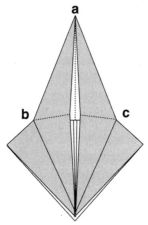

**9.** Lift just the top layer of the paper at point **a**. Think of this as opening a frog's mouth. Open it up and back to line **b-c**. Crease the line **b-c inside** the frog's mouth.

Press on points **b** and **c** to **reverse** the folds along lines **a-b** and **a-c**. The trick is to get the paper to lie flat in the long diamond shape shown on the right. At first it will seem impossible. Have patience.

**10–13.** Turn the paper over. **Repeat** Steps 6 to 9 on this side. When you have finished, your paper will look like the diamond to the right with two "legs" at the bottom.

**14 & 15.** Taper the diamond at its legs by folding the **top** layer of each side in the direction of the arrows along lines **a-f** and **a-e** so that they meet at the center line.

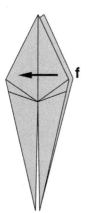

**16 & 17.** Turn the paper over. **Repeat** Steps 14 and 15 on this side to complete the tapering of the two legs.

**18.** The figure to the left has two skinny legs. Lift the **upper** flap at point **f** (be sure it's just the upper flap) and fold it over in the direction of the arrow—as if turning the page of a book. This is called a "book fold."

Turn the entire figure over.

**19.** Repeat this "book fold" (Step 18) on this side. Be sure to fold over only the **top** "page."

**20.** The figure to the right looks like a fox with two pointy ears at the top and a pointy nose at the bottom. Open the **upper** layer of the fox's mouth at point **a**, and crease it along line **g-h** so that the fox's nose touches the top of the fox's ears.

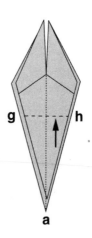

**21.** Turn the figure over. **Repeat** Step 20 on this side so that all four points touch.

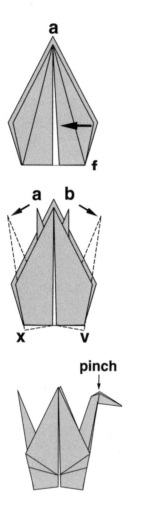

**22.** Now for another "book fold." Lift the **top** layer of the figure to the left (at point **f**) and fold it in the direction of the arrow.

**23.** Turn the entire figure over. **Repeat** the "book fold" (Step 22) on this side.

**24 & 25.** There are two points, **a** and **b**, below the upper flap. Pull out each one, in the direction of the arrows, as far as the dotted lines. Press down along the base (at points **x** and **y**) to make them stay in place.

**26.** Take the end of one of the points and bend it down to make the head of the crane. Using your thumbnail, **reverse** the crease in the head, and **pinch** it to form the beak. The other point becomes the tail.

**27.** Open the body by blowing into the hole underneath the crane and then gently pulling out the wings. And there it is!

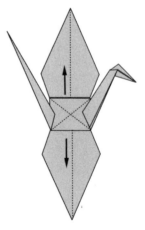

# About the Author

Naomi Hirahara grew up in Southern California speaking both Japanese and English. After graduating from college with a degree in international relations, she lived for a year in Japan, where she was able to spend some time with her maternal grandmother and other relatives. A mystery writer and former journalist, she won an Edgar Allan Poe Award for *Snakeskin Shamisen*, her third book in the Mas Arai adult mystery series. Her favorite words include *pneuma* and *kuru-kuru-pa*. Visit her at www.1001cranesbook.com or www.naomihira hara.com.